THE WICCAN'S CIRCLE

THE WICCAN SAGA
BOOK 3

AYLA VOLK

PREFACE

The Wiccan's Circle is the third book of The Wiccan Saga, a paranormal shifter romance series. For the best reading experience, it is recommended to read this series sequentially. Recommended reading age is 18+.

1

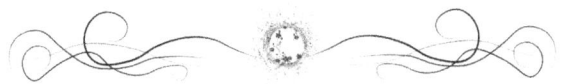

Juniper

I gripped the worn leather reins tightly as excitement filled me. I glanced back at Forest, who looked far less thrilled with the idea of riding horses than I was.

"We have horses back home," I teased him.

"Yeah, but I leave them to Oliver and the others to handle."

I could hear Caspian chuckle as he lifted himself onto his saddle.

"We find it a better tactic to herd the cattle with horses. Since it is our main source of income, we all participate." He looked at me, "Make sure you don't hold those too tight. The horse will feel the tension."

I lessened my hold on the straps, eager to learn. We had been at my father's pack for a few days. Both he and June, his mate, had given us the grand tour of their land. Today, we were helping move some of their cattle up to another pasture. Besides the three of us, there were a handful of Silver Ridge men heading up with us.

"Alpha Forest and yourself will stay in the back with me. We will let the others take up the sides," Caspian told me.

"Sounds good," I smiled back at him.

He let out a sharp whistle, and everyone began moving. Snow still stuck to the shadows of the tree line, but the warmth of spring had melted it from the center of the greening meadows. It took Forest and me a few minutes to get used to riding, but the horses seemed to know what they were doing. We followed the herd of black cattle up a beautiful valley. A serpentining sapphire blue river flowed down the center, surrounded by a thick sea of emerald green grass that dissipated as the trees took over. The pine-covered mountains sloped upwards on either side of the valley, casting shadows on the glen below. It looked like a scene straight out of a movie. The beauty and perfection seemed as if only fiction could have created it, yet here we were. I took all of it in, savoring every moment of the experience.

After nearly two hours of riding, the sun began to take hold against the shadows as the trees opened up, revealing a thriving meadow. The first colors of spring wildflowers sprinkled the landscape as bees made themselves busy with their work collecting pollen for their hives, darting from one bloom to the next.

"Right up here," Caspian called out.

The Silver Ridge men whistled and ran their horses, directing the cattle across the shallow river into their fresh feeding grounds. I watched, mesmerized, as they moved them with ease.

"I wanted to show you two something while we were here," Caspian told us. "Let's go up this way."

He led us towards the hills, breaking back into the towering trees. A narrow dirt trail looped its way through. I listened to the birds singing overhead and closed my eyes as I took a deep breath in. The air was crisp and fresh. I could smell the first of the flowers that had welcomed the warming weather.

"Where are we heading?" Forest asked him.

"You'll see when we get there," Caspian smiled back.

We started heading up the mountain through switchbacks that zigged and zagged up the slope. A part of me wished I could jump off of the horse so that I could be closer to the ground. I felt like I was missing so much from atop it.

"My father used to bring me up here all the time when I was a boy. It's my favorite spot on all of our land."

"I can't wait to see what it is," I told Caspian.

I could hear the crashing of water ahead of us. Caspian held up his hand, signaling that we should stop.

"We can unload here," he said as he dismounted from his steed.

He tied the horse to a branch nearby and walked back to hold onto mine as I followed suit. Forest dropped off his own horse and tied it up by the other two.

"Just a little further," Caspian pointed up the trail.

I was excited to be down on the trail with my own two feet as I took in my surroundings. With the strengthening sound of water, I picked up my pace, unable to hold myself back. We turned a corner, revealing a massive waterfall cascading down a rocky cliff face. A rippling pool of steel blue water sat at the bottom of the falls.

"It's beautiful," I gushed.

"I thought you might think so," Caspian smiled at me.

"Can I swim here?"

"It's probably pretty chilly. It's all snow melt."

"That won't be a problem for her," Forest told him as he watched me with amusement.

I started stripping off my clothes, nearly tripping on them as the eagerness took hold.

"Next time, give your old man a heads up," Caspian called over.

I looked back at him to see he had turned away. Forest stood beside him with his arms crossed over his chest, chuckling. I finished undressing and dove into the water. I could feel the strong flow of power pull into my body. I swam towards the crashing waters and dove underneath. It felt like an electrical charge revitalizing every inch of me. I came up on the back side of the falls and held myself tight to the smoothed granite rock face. I ran my hand up the stone, finding a good hold to steady myself as I bent my head backward, allowing the water to run through my hair. I could have stayed there all day, hidden away in a sanctuary amongst the water. When I turned around, I could see the shadows of Caspian and Forest coming to the pool's edge.

"Juniper," Caspian called out.

I could barely make out his voice past the thundering waters next to me. I dove back under and popped my head up on the other side.

"Juniper, I've been calling for you," Caspian worriedly expressed.

"I told you, she does that," Forest said from beside him, unfazed.

I smiled at him, "I'm sorry, I could barely hear you. I was on the other side of the falls."

I swam closer to the edge where they were standing.

"I take it you like water?" Caspian asked.

I leaned back into the natural pool, "I love it. It gives me energy."

"Her witch side," Forrest explained. "She absorbs the energy and power from the water."

Caspian ran his hand through his thick brown hair, "I guess that makes sense."

"It takes some getting used to. At home, I can't keep her away from the glacial lakes."

"I guess I chose right bringing you here."

"Oh, yes. This is truly amazing. I haven't had an opportunity to swim under such a powerful waterfall before. It's invigorating."

Caspian chuckled, "I'm glad you like it."

"You might want to settle in," Forest added, "I don't foresee Juniper getting out of there anytime soon."

Caspian nodded and took a seat on a rock outcropping nearby. I dove back under, swimming up the current. I stopped to look at the trout swimming by some nearby rocks. Their steady movements kept them in place against the water's pull. I enjoyed watching them and took note of their graceful, speckled colors.

It must have been nearly an hour before I made my way back to the side of the pool. Forest stood there with a blanket held out to wrap me in.

"You brought a blanket?" I asked, surprised.

"Caspian had one in his satchel."

"Never go without it," he hollered from the trees.

"Thank you," I called back to him.

I dried off and redressed, slightly disappointed to leave, but I didn't want the others to have to wait on me any longer. I could have spent the entire day there. As we rode back down the way we had come, I felt renewed and ready to take on the rest of the day. When we arrived back at the barn, several men came out and took our horses from us.

"June has lunch ready at the pack house if you both are hungry," Caspian offered.

"I'm starved. Thank you for taking us up with you," I smiled at him.

"Thank you for going along with me."

We joined the rest of the Silver Ridge Pack, along with our own warriors, as we ate a hearty lunch of chili and cornbread. It was the perfect meal after the morning ride. The Silver Ridge Pack ate most of their meals together in a large dining room in the pack house. It was served cafeteria style, where everyone lined up at the kitchen window to receive their serving. Of course, the high-ranked wolves, including ourselves, were served at our table. We were sitting with Caspian and June.

"How was your ride this morning?" June inquired.

"It was amazing! Caspian took us up to the most beautiful waterfall," I told her.

"It is beautiful up there, isn't it? He took me there when we first mated. I never tire of it."

"I don't think you ever can," I smiled warmly at her.

"What's in store for the rest of the day?" Forest asked Caspian.

"I need to attend to some things in-house, but you and your pack are welcome to wander around and see what you can find."

"I'm heading into town to get some supplies if you want to join?" June added.

I looked over at Forest to see if he had a preference. He shrugged his shoulders at me, his go-to sign for letting me decide.

"We would love to join you, June. Thank you for the offer."

"Great! We can head out right after lunch."

Just as she promised, we loaded into her large suburban after lunch and started on our way. I decided to ride with June while Forest and August followed behind in their car.

"It's nice to have just us girls," she smiled at me as she drove off of pack lands.

"It is. Do you go into town often?" I asked her.

"Once or twice a week. It depends on how much everyone eats back at home. You know those men. They can put it away," she laughed.

"I never realized how much one being could eat until I joined the West Moon Pack."

"It's a give-away for our kind—hearty eaters," she smiled as she turned down a road.

"My boys don't like to join me too often. They always feel like their job is to be by their father's side, but as Lunas, we know that caring for the pack includes more than protection. Each person needs to be cared for from the bottom up."

I took in her wisdom, thinking of ways I could do better for my own pack. The drive was fairly quick, just short of half an hour to get to the town. Old painted wooden and brick buildings lined the main street with mountains on all sides. It was picturesque. We pulled into the parking lot of a small grocery store on the far end of town and unloaded. Forest parked in the spot next to us.

"You two are welcome to join or take a look around if you want. We won't be too long," June told them as they exited their vehicle.

"We will go take a walk in town and meet back up with you here in about twenty minutes," Forest replied.

I gave him a quick kiss before following June into the store. She pulled a cart out and passed it to me before pulling another for herself. I had only been to a grocery store once before when I still lived at the coven. I had gone with my Gran to get some ingredients that had been forgotten on our weekly grocery delivery. I looked across the ample space, taking in the aisles of the food and produce section around me. Bright fluorescents shined overhead, ensuring no corner was left in shadow.

"Do you shop for everything that the ranch uses?" I asked her.

"Some of the workers come themselves to get things, but since we feed them all in the main house, I do the bulk of the shopping. I have a standing order that I pick up once a week, but on days like today, I come to get some extras to tide us over until our normal pick-up day."

We walked towards the produce and started bagging apples, oranges, and a variety of other fruits and vegetables that they had in good stock. Before I knew it, June's whole cart was full.

"We get most of our produce from the store. Dry goods I get in bulk from the larger cities, and meat we cover at home," she explained.

We went down one of the aisles, and she began to fill my cart with juices and soda. We grabbed a few things down another couple of aisles before heading to the register.

"Good afternoon, Mrs. June," the cashier said as she rang us up.

"Hi there, Carol. How are your grandbabies doing?"

"Oh, you know how the little ones are. Busy as always."

"You're telling me. I miss when my boys were that young. Now they always have their own things to fill their time."

"Just wait until you have grandbabies of your own."

"I have a few years yet," she smiled back at the elderly woman.

We pushed our carts back to the cars and began loading the supplies into the back of her car. Once it had all been put away, we walked over to Main Street to look for Forest and August. Most of the buildings contained mom-and-pop shops or small restaurants. There was an old stone church near the center that I stopped to admire.

"This is an old mining town, so most of the buildings are from the late eighteen hundreds and early nineteen hundreds. A few have been rebuilt or fixed up over time, but they try and keep the same aesthetic. More younger couples have been moving in and trying to modernize the shops. They've added some clothing stores and even a 'chic' dog store," she informed me.

"What's a chic dog store?" I asked her with curiosity.

"It's all posh homemade dog treats and designer collars. They're cute, but I think they've set up in the wrong market. Most of the people around here with dogs are ranchers. No one is willing to spend that kind of money on their working dogs, though they do have some nice meat-covered bones, I suppose."

From my time living amongst the pack, I saw how shifters looked at pet stores. Watching dogs collared and leashed paraded around by humans could hit a raw nerve to some, though I still didn't have a problem with it. The dogs people owned were far different from what we turned into.

We found Forest and August walking out of a small store. Forest had a brown bag in his hand.

"Did you do a little shopping?" I asked him teasingly.

"I thought I would get you a souvenir from our trip."

He pulled out a long black dress made from soft cotton. The bottom had layers sewn together as they tapered down. It was in my 'hippy' style, as he called it.

"Thank you," I smiled at him as I looked it over. "It's beautiful."

We stopped at the little cafe and grabbed a drink before returning to the Silver Ridge Pack.

2

Juniper

Whet we pulled up in front of the Silver Ridge pack house, several people came out from within to help unload the car. So many hands made quick work putting all of the groceries we had purchased away, and I soon found my way into the kitchen, where June was rolling up her sleeves to start preparing dinner.

"Do you help with all of the meals?" I asked her.

"Most. I love cooking and enjoy taking care of our pack. Do you ever help at your home?"

"Most of the pack eat at the diner or in their homes. In the pack house, we have a cook, so there aren't too many opportunities to help out. However, where I grew up, I often helped my Gran prepare meals for our family, but I never took the lead."

"Why don't I show you what we do here," she offered—a hint of excitement in her eyes.

"I would love that. Thank you," I replied eagerly.

I washed up and joined her at the counter. She had several jars of aromatic dried spices in front of her, along with a large bowl.

"Since we serve so many, we make things in bulk. Today, we are going to make our meat rub. First, we will add the spices and some salt and pepper."

She handed me a measuring cup and a large jar of garlic powder. We quickly went to work adding and mixing each spice to the bowl. Bryony, one of the other girls who worked in the kitchen, brought over the first tray of steaks.

June grabbed one and tossed it on her board, "Now we rub the spices onto the meat. Make sure you cover the entire steak."

I followed her directions carefully. When I looked over, I saw that she had already nearly completed the tray of steaks, whereas I had only done five.

"You're fast!" I gawked at her.

"You get used to it. You learn how to massage it in, covering the whole steak. Speed is not important; it is the care you give to it."

Bryony brought a second tray while collecting the first. I enjoyed spending this time with June. The more time I spent with her, the more comfortable I became. This had been my first trip to meet my father's pack and family. I had been hesitant the first few days since I was his illegitimate daughter, but they had welcomed me with open arms. We only had two days left before we needed to return to our pack, and I was determined to make the most of it.

After prepping the steaks, we moved on to peeling potatoes. June's three sons came into the kitchen, snagging bits of food off the counter.

"You boys head on out of here," June warned them.

"We're hungry, Mom," Cain, the youngest, protested. "And we don't have anything to do."

Jasper swatted his brother on the shoulder and looked warily at June.

"Nothing to do, huh?" June said with mischief in her voice. "Perhaps you want to take Juniper out and show her around? You boys should get to know your sister better anyway."

I froze at her sudden suggestion. I didn't want to feel like an inconvenience for them.

"They don't need to if they don't want to. Besides, I'm helping you," I offered, hoping not to become a burden to them.

June pushed her fist into her hip, and she cocked an eyebrow and a knowing smirk, "Nonsense. You four have not had much time to get to know each other. It is important for you all to get to know each other better, just as we have."

She eyed her boys in a warning.

"Of course, mom. We can take her out," Jasper, the oldest, said unemotionally.

"Okay," I said hesitantly.

I washed off my hands and grabbed my jacket from a nearby chair before we filed out the back door. We walked silently down a dirt trail through a meadow, nearing the crowded tree line.

"Where should we go?" Cain asked as we walked.

Jasper, who was leading us, stopped and turned to look at us.

"What do you think Oliver?"

Oliver seemed like the quiet one of the bunch as he simply shrugged.

"You guys don't really need to take me out if you don't want to," I offered.

"What? And miss spending time with our witch sister?" Cain joked as he jumped from one foot to the other.

I tensed slightly at the word witch but let it slide, not wanting to make a big deal of it. I was a witch, after all. I just wasn't used to people saying it aloud. Only a second later, Jasper slapped Cain upside the back of his head.

"What was that for?" Cain protested, rubbing the back of his head.

Jasper rolled his eyes at his brother.

"Sorry about him. It's not a problem to take you out," Jasper said.

"Okay," I replied hesitantly.

"Let's take her up to the old mine," Oliver finally replied to Jasper's original question.

"What's the old mine?" I asked them as we started walking again.

"It's an old silver mine from back during the gold rush," Oliver explained.

"It's so cool. You can even see where the old town used to be," Cain added.

"That sounds great. Is it far?"

"A few miles. We can shift if you prefer?" Jasper added.

"Whatever you guys want."

I preferred to hike. I liked being able to take my time on a trail, but I didn't want to be more of an inconvenience than I already felt. They were all teenage boys, with Jasper being the eldest at nineteen and Cain only fourteen. Cain and Oliver had been at school all day, and I was sure they didn't want to spend their little free time taking me on a sightseeing tour.

"We will hike then. Cain hasn't shifted yet, and I would prefer not to carry him on my back if I don't have to."

"Sounds good to me," I replied.

"Hey, I only have a few more years, and then I will be faster than both of you!" Cain shouted and laughed at them.

"Sure you will," Jasper said back at him with a smile teasing the corner of his mouth. He seemed to like to give his brothers a hard time, but he truly enjoyed their antics.

We followed the winding trail through the forest, climbing higher up one of the mountains.

"What do you guys usually do when you're not playing tour guide?" I asked them.

"We are usually training with our dad or the warriors," Jasper answered.

"Why not today?"

"Our dad had a meeting with the Beta. Sometimes, he has us join, but not always. They are usually boring anyway, so we don't mind missing out," Olivier explained.

"How do you like training with him?"

"It's fine. We've been doing it all our lives. Since I finished school, it has become my main job. I'm basically his shadow, following him to observe how he handles pack matters."

"When will you take over as Alpha?"

"Probably not for another ten or twenty years," Jasper shrugged.

"That's a long time to train for it."

"It's a big responsibility."

I thought of my own role within my pack back home. I was the Luna. I had come to learn that most high-ranking daughters would be trained on the different responsibilities of being a Luna as well as Beta and Gamma females. June had explained to me earlier in the week that she had been the daughter of an Alpha of a nearby pack. She had been trained since she was only five on how to fulfill the role. I had only stepped into this world nine months ago. It made me question if I was doing everything I was supposed to be.

We broke through the trees to a small meadow. "Look," Cain called as he ran over to a row of stones hidden within the tall grass. "This was one of the old buildings."

"Wow, that's so neat," I exclaimed as I examined them. "Are there a lot of them?"

"Yeah. I've found ten buildings so far. And that," he pointed up the mountain to a dilapidated wooden frame with a pile of rocks falling down the hillside from within, "is the mine."

"That's just the tailings," Oliver corrected him.

"What are tailings?" I asked.

"It's where they dumped the rock they mined out. The entrance is around the side," Oliver explained.

We wandered around the clearing. Cain pointed out each of the old foundations hidden amongst the wild grass before we headed up towards the opening of the mine. As we curved a corner, some still-standing wooden buildings stood against the forested area. You could see what once were old rail tracks leading into one of the buildings. It was made from thick wood, and portions had caved in over its years of abuse from the elements. We climbed inside through an opening and looked at the wooden pillars and metal that still stood before following the tracks out and up to the mine's entrance.

"Damn, we didn't grab any flashlights," Jasper said to no one in particular.

"Can't we see with our wolves?" I asked them.

"It's completely black in there. Even our wolves can't help us."

"I can help," I offered after seeing their disappointment.

They looked at me quizzically, but soon, their expressions shifted to anticipation.

"Like you said, I am a witch," I winked at them.

"That's so cool!" Cain shouted with excitement.

We stood at the entrance of the darkened mine. I rubbed my hands together and held one out, palm up, as I began to chant.

"Cumhachd a-staigh, sruthadh troimhe, soillsich solas romham."

A flame formed at the center of my hand. I repeated my chant a few more times, helping it grow larger. I looked up at the others when it was the size I wanted. Cain's face was elated with excitement, while Oliver and Jasper looked amused, but I could tell they were trying to hide their excitement.

"Shall we?" I asked them.

Jasper led us into the mine shaft, followed by myself, Cain, and Oliver. With the fire in my hand illuminating the area, we could make out the old timber supports and rough compacted dirt walls. The cart tracks led down the center of the shaft. As we traveled further, I tripped over an old pick axe on the ground. Jasper caught my arm and steadied me before I could fall. I gave him a quick thanks but was cut off by a swarm of bats startled by the screech I had let out and flew toward us. We all ducked down out of their way. I could feel the wind whip by me from their movement. The stagnate smell of old water and dirt grew stronger as they brought the air from the belly of the cave to us.

"Are you alright?" Jasper asked me.

I looked back where the bats had flown before answering, "I'm fine. They just startled me."

"Maybe they thought you were calling to them," Cain joked.

My cheeks flushed with embarrassment, but Oliver shoved his brother while Jasper shook his head.

"You will learn to ignore him," Jasper chastised his brother.

"My cousin, who I grew up with, is like him," I smiled at them. "I can handle it."

The thought of Meadow and how we last parted brought sadness to me. After her mother's death and her grandmother's banishment from our coven, she had come to stay with us for a month at West Moon. It was good for her to find some happiness again, but it made her not want to return home. We had fought over it. If she did not return to the coven, she too would be banished, and I would not be allowed to talk to her again. We hadn't spoken since, and every time I thought of her, my heart broke into pieces again.

Jasper pulled me from my thoughts, "What is your cousin like?"

"She is really my second cousin, but she was more like a sister to me. We are the same age and grew up nearly inseparable."

"Do you still see your family from...that side?" he asked.

"I do. I try to visit them every couple of months."

"What was it like growing up in a coven?"

"Different..." I started. "For one, there were only women. Men were not allowed at our home besides the occasional handyman."

"That's what I'm talking about," Cain chimed in, raising his eyebrows repeatedly.

I ignored him as I continued, "Everything was about the land and nature. We farmed and gathered. We set traps for our meat and shopped for what we could not collect or make ourselves."

"Sounds pretty similar to us," Oliver murmured.

"I suppose, in that way, it is. And the community. We were all very close. My family has fifteen women; most live in our main house, while a few have houses of their own. My Grandmother raised me after my mother died."

"Our dad mentioned that she died. I'm sorry about that," Jasper told me as we continued down the shaft. "How did it happen?"

"She was murdered."

I could sense their eyes on me. It was always a big story when it was brought up, and I didn't feel like sharing it again. Perhaps another time, but right now, I wanted to enjoy my time with my newfound brothers, not live in the past.

"What about you guys? How was it being raised as the Alpha's children?" I quickly asked, steering the conversation elsewhere.

"Great!" Cain said smugly.

"It's a lot of responsibility," Jasper added. "There is a higher standard on how we behave. If our friends wanted to go out and get into mischief, we had to stay back."

"Except that one time you and Gavin got caught past the border," Oliver said.

"Shut it," Jasper glared at him in warning.

"Oh, come on, Jasper," Cain goaded him. "It's not that bad. Tell her the story."

"It's nothing," he spoke as he started walking ahead.

"He's just embarrassed that he got in trouble. He's the

golden boy," Cain said as he walked back up to Jasper, throwing an arm over his shoulder.

"What about you?" I asked Oliver.

He shrugged, "Like Jasper said, it's a lot of responsibility. We train more. When we aren't training, we usually work with our father or one of the other high ranks. It wasn't so bad when we were kids. We were allowed to play with the rest of the kids. Our dad goes on about how he wants us to be prepared early since he had to take over so young. I'm sure he felt overwhelmed and is trying to prevent that from happening to us."

"Forest took over young, too. I can see where he is coming from."

Oliver nodded but didn't reply. We caught back up to Cain and Jasper as the shaft finally opened. Old wooden boxes were stacked against the side of the room, and tools were scattered around. I heard a crunch beneath my foot as I stepped on a broken piece of glass.

"Careful," Jasper warned.

I pulled my foot back off the glass and carefully placed it down to the side of it.

"There are a bunch of tunnels leading out from here. We've been down most of them. A few are underwater now," Oliver explained.

"What have you guys found in here?"

"It is mostly what you see around here. There are some old explosives down one of the tunnels," Jasper explained.

"How often do you guys come up here?"

"Not as much anymore. We used to love coming up as kids to explore."

"Our dad hates it, though," Cain smiled. "He says the mines are too dangerous."

Oh, great. Just what I needed was to anger my father after I first met him. Yet, I was happy that my brothers were willing to share this with me.

"Why do you guys like it up here so much?"

They just shrugged their shoulders.

"It's a place to explore," Cain finally said. "Who doesn't like doing that?"

We looked around the room for a while, checking out all the long-lost treasures left behind. It was like a time capsule —a look into a long-forgotten time. There was even an old pair of boots in one of the corners. I could only imagine the story they could tell. After a short while, we decided to make our way back out. I wasn't sure how long my fire would hold out as I had never kept it lit for so long. As we broke out of the darkness, we saw a breathtaking sunset in front of us. The bright orange sky warmed me from within with its beauty.

"We should head back for dinner," Jasper said.

We started walking back down the mountainside when I saw all three of my brothers stop in their tracks.

"What's wrong?" I asked them.

"Rogues..."

3

Juniper

Forest, *where are you?* I linked my mate.

The warriors and I are running to the east. What's wrong?

"Where are the rogues?" I asked Jasper.

"To the south."

Rogues, to the south, I shared the information with him.

Stay at the pack house. We will head that way to help out. Let your father know.

"Tell your dad that Forest and the warriors are on their way to help."

I thought about telling Forest where I was, but I knew he would come to me instead, and I didn't want to worry him. He would want to help. We were on the other side of the pack's territory anyway.

"I have to go help," Jasper told us. "I let my dad know about Alpha Forest. Oliver, you take Juniper and Cain back to the pack house."

"I should help too," Oliver protested.

"You need to carry Cain. Get back quickly."

I could tell Oliver was frustrated but didn't argue back against his brother. Jasper shifted, shredding his clothes, and took off down the mountain. I looked back at the other two.

"Should we shift?" I asked.

"Yeah..." Oliver replied, watching his brother's dark brown wolf as he ran through the trees.

I took the lead and turned away from them before pulling my shirt over my head. While nudity was not something people found taboo within packs or even my coven, they were still my brothers, and I had only just met them. I set my shirt on the ground and unclasped my bra, laying it onto the shirt, and then continued with my jeans and shoes. I quickly tied it together to carry it back and shifted, picking up my makeshift bag in my jaws. When I turned around, my brothers were facing away from me. Oliver had shifted into a nearly identical brown wolf to his brother's, though he was smaller. I yipped at them to signal that I was ready. They looked back at my red wolf.

"Did you make a bag?" Cain teased.

I let out a low growl, warning him not to poke the wolf, but he smiled even more prominently and climbed on his brother's back, clutching Oliver's clothes. We started down the trail, moving quickly yet carefully since Oliver was carrying Cain. When we returned to the trail, we raced to the pack house as promptly as our paws would take us.

Forest

WE RACED to the southern border, listening for signs of a skirmish. I had four of my warriors and August with me. We had gone for a run to fit in some training while Juniper was busy with June. I had wanted them to have some time together to bond. When she had linked me that there were rogues at the border, I quickly rallied my men to help. I was sure the Silver Ridge Pack could handle it, but this pack was now related to me, and I would not shy away from fighting to protect them. If anything happened to Juniper's father, it would hurt her, and I would not tolerate that.

We heard growling up ahead of us and ran straight for it. Caspian came into view. He was standing in his human form, yelling at a man across the trees. I immediately recognized the other man as Callan, the Silver Ridge warrior who had caused a fight in the bar back at West Moon. His disheveled look and sour scent told me what had come to be from that skirmish. Caspian had said to me that he would put him on trial when they returned home, but I never heard the outcome. Now, I knew that he had been banished. That or he left, which I highly doubted. We stayed in the trees, giving them space, but we listened to the conversation.

"This is the last time I will warn you to stay away from the pack, Callan. You are banished, a rogue. We do not take kindly to rogues, and you know it," Caspian warned him.

"Look at the mighty Alpha now. If you were so strong and powerful, why let me live? I won't stop coming back until I have my mate."

"Your mate was not banished. She chose to stay on her own, and we will respect that."

"She belongs to me!" Callan yelled at him.

"She belongs with the Silver Ridge Pack. If she wanted to

be with you, she would go to you. Leave now, or I won't be so kind."

Callan let out a deep growl before shifting and running back into the forest behind him. Caspian ran his hand through his hair and turned around, spotting me.

"Alpha Forest, thank you for lending a hand."

I shifted so that we could speak.

"Trouble with your old warrior?"

"Yes. He wants his mate back, but she chooses to stay. She is part of my pack. I will protect her no matter what."

I nodded in understanding. I could see Callan's mark on his shoulder as he argued with Caspian. He and his mate had completed their mating, which meant that if Caspian were to kill Callan, he would kill his mate as well. It was a difficult situation to be in. I was honestly a little surprised that whoever the woman was, she had not gone with him. The separation would not be easy on either of them.

"Is there anything we can help you with?"

"No. We must resolve this situation ourselves, but I thank you for your offer."

"It is a standing offer if you change your mind."

He nodded at me, "Come, dinner should be ready."

We shifted back and returned to the pack house. I was eager to see Juniper. Anytime a potential threat came to hand, my wolf yearned to check on her. My heart instantly warmed when I found her standing out front with June waiting for us. Her beauty was radiant. I shifted back, and she handed me a pair of pants to slide on, followed by a shirt.

"Is everything alright?" She asked, concerned.

"Everything is fine," Caspian answered. "It's just some troubles with an old pack member."

I could see June shake her head in disapproval.

"An old pack member?" Juniper questioned further.

June informed her, "It's just an old warrior who has a hard time being on the outside. There's nothing to worry about. Let's get these men fed."

Juniper smiled at her and held my hand as we walked into the pack house, searching for dinner. The invading smell of steak and potatoes was a welcomed surprise. We took our seats at the table, and two pack members came up with our plates in hand.

"Thank you, Bryony," June said as her plate was set down.

"You made my favorite," Caspian looked at his mate lovingly.

"I thought you would be in the mood for it," she smiled back.

I looked over at Juniper, who watched them with adoration. Caspian's three sons joined us at the table. The middle child, Oliver, shoved his younger brother before they sat down. Three alpha boys were sure to be a handful, but I was impressed with how well Caspian and June handled them.

"How was your outing?" June asked them.

"It was good," Jasper, the eldest, replied unemotionally.

"Well...where did you go?"

I watched as he flitted his eyes for a quick second over to Cain before replying, "We took her up the north mountain."

"Yeah, we showed her the old mine camp," Cain said.

"You boys better have stayed out of that mine," Caspian warned.

"Of course," Cain said with a cocky smile.

They had most definitely gone into the mine they had spoken of. I could tell that Caspian didn't believe them one bit. He looked over them, watching for any sign of their deceit.

"You had better not have taken her up there," June spoke low in an angered voice.

All eyes, including my own, shot over to Juniper, who looked uncomfortable in her seat.

"They showed me the old foundations. Ten, right? There were ten of them," she said quickly before looking at her brothers.

She was a terrible liar.

"I didn't realize you had gone with your brothers," I asked her.

I wanted to know more about what she had been up to, but at the same time, I wanted to save her from the awkward situation. She should not lie to another alpha, even her father.

"Uh, yeah. June thought it would be a good idea for us to bond."

"It was a good idea," June said as she stared her boys down, "I should have known better than to trust them not to get you in trouble. How often do we have to tell you three how dangerous that mine is? It can cave in at any time. What would happen if you all were hurt?"

The more information I got, the more angry I became. Had they endangered my mate? It took everything in me to bite my tongue and not lash out at the three adolescents for their poor decision.

"I expected more from you, Jasper. You will be Alpha one day, and here you are, endangering not only your sister but a visiting Luna," Caspian lectured him.

They were both speaking quietly so as not to gain the attention of the surrounding pack members, but I could see the heads from the tables closest to us turning in our direction.

"Perhaps this is a conversation best held later?" I suggested.

I didn't feel chastising the future Alpha before the pack was a good idea. It could lead to a lack of support for him in the future. Caspian took a deep breath.

"I want the three of you in my office after dinner. Do you understand?"

"Yes, Alpha," they all responded, lowering their heads and using his title.

They knew they were in trouble.

"They were really great with me. I'm sorry if I caused any problems," Juniper tried to defend them.

Caspian's face softened when he looked at her.

"While I appreciate your kind words about my sons, they knew better, and we will discuss this later."

I watched as Juniper whispered an apology at them before looking back down at her food. I could feel her anxiousness through our bond and watched as she moved her food around the plate. I held her thigh under the table, offering her support. She forced a smile at me, but her unease continued. After dinner, Juniper and I walked back up to our room.

"I don't want them to get in trouble," she told me when we were safely away from prying ears. "Is there anything we can do?"

"They shouldn't have taken you up there," I told her. The slight swell of anger that they were putting her at risk nipped at the edges of my mind, but I eased it back.

"It was a great bonding moment, Forest. They told me

how they always went up there as kids and shared that with me."

"It doesn't matter. If Caspian believes the mines are dangerous, everyone must respect that decision. We are guests on their land. If you try to get in the middle, it could cause problems."

"Am I supposed to be a part of their family? Surely, he would let me speak to him."

I wasn't sure how to respond to her. Although she was technically part of their family, she was blood, but she had not grown up with them or their customs. They did things differently from even our pack. Politics were always tricky regarding relations between packs, but Juniper's relationship with her father was even more complex in understanding what would be considered appropriate.

"The best thing to do until we know Caspian and his pack better is to let him handle it as he sees fit. Questioning how an Alpha handles a situation can be considered an insult. I don't want you to get off on the wrong foot with them."

"This stinks," she whined as she plopped on the bed.

"It does, but you're a strong Luna. You will figure it out in time."

She sat up straight, "You're right. I am."

She jumped off the bed and headed to the door.

"Where are you going?"

"To talk to my father."

4

Juniper

I walked down the stairs and headed straight to the offices. I wished I could hear what was happening behind the closed door. I clenched my fists, gaining the bravery I needed to address my father. I was a Luna, and it would only be fair for him to listen to me. I should be able to speak up for my brothers. I knocked twice and took a small step back. After a moment, Caspian opened the door. His stern look softened when he looked down at me.

"Juniper, I didn't expect you," he said, surprised.

I chewed on my lip for a moment before replying, "Do you have a moment to talk?"

"Sure, come on in," he smiled softly at me.

He held the door open, and I saw all three of my brothers seated on the sofas with their heads down.

"You three can go, but remember what we spoke of," he said sternly.

"Yes, Alpha," they replied before they passed us, leaving the room.

I forced a smile at them, but none returned my look. Caspian closed the door, and we sat back on the sofas.

"Can I get you a drink?" He offered.

"No, thank you."

"What can I do for you?"

"I know it may not be my place, but I had hoped that I could talk you into going light on your boys."

Caspian sat back and draped his arm over the back of the dark brown leather sofa—small creases forming to the weight.

The corner of his mouth tilted lightly as he looked at me with a smirk, "Really? Why would you ask that?"

"The boys did indeed take me to the mine. I understand you feel it is dangerous, but they wanted to share something special with me. I was so appreciative that they included me; I would hate to see them punished for it."

"There are many special things that they could have shared with you. The mines are dangerous. They could have been hurt, or even worse, you could have been hurt," he said more seriously.

"I understand, but we could have been injured from doing anything, really. They made sure to take care of me, and we did not go too far into the mine," I pushed further, hoping it wasn't past the breaking point.

"I have to say that I like seeing you four come together, though I don't approve of the methods," he added. "You truly are a Luna."

I smiled at him, "Why do you say that?"

"You want to protect those you care about. The way you

go about it, well...it is fitting of a Luna. Most would be terrified to come to ask that of an Alpha."

"I must admit, I had hoped I had some brownie points for being your daughter as well."

He laughed loudly before responding, "I would say you do."

"So does that mean you will take it easy on them?" I asked hopefully.

"I have already told them that they will have to get up early for extra training before school. What do you suppose I should do with them instead?"

I thought momentarily, "Perhaps they can take me out again? But not to the mines."

"You leave the day after tomorrow."

"So after school tomorrow it is," I smiled broadly at him.

He chuckled, "I will leave it to you to tell them."

"I would be happy to," I beamed.

We sat and talked for a few more minutes. Before I told them the good news, Caspian still wanted the boys to sulk for a while. I said goodnight to my father, who pointed me toward where I would find my brothers.

I walked down the hallway to a rec room in the back of the house. All three of them were engrossed in a video game on the television. I leaned on the door frame, watching as their characters darted through the streets, shooting at others.

"Is this really what you do for fun?" I cracked at them.

They paused their game and turned toward me.

"What are you doing here?" Jasper asked in his unemotional voice that I had become familiar with.

"Figured I would let you know that I got you out of your training in the morning."

"What!" Cain shouted as he jumped from his seat, his excitement evident. "How did you do that?"

"Well, I hope you don't mind that I asked if, instead, you guys could take me out again after school tomorrow."

"We have training after school," Oliver noted.

"Not if you take me out..."

"No way! You're the best!" Cain shouted as he pumped his arms in the air.

"What did you say to get him to change his mind?" Jasper asked suspiciously.

"I just talked to him. I guess sometimes it pays to have a sister," I offered up, not knowing what else to say.

"Yeah, one that's a Luna," Cain added. "He has to listen to you."

"I think if you talk to him, he would be understanding," I told them.

"I think it's different for you," Jasper said.

I wasn't quite sure if he was mad at me or not. I felt like the best thing to do was level with them. I could already tell they didn't like beating around the bush.

"It is. I didn't have him growing up, but you did. You guys know everything about him as he does for you. You know how to push each other's buttons, but every time I speak to him and you, I feel like I have to walk on eggshells. Remember, I didn't grow up in a pack. I don't know what I can and cannot say to other alphas, let alone another alpha, who is my father. I was terrified going in there, but you three are my brothers, and I knew I needed to try. For you."

They each looked over at me with a slight look of admiration in their eyes.

"We can take you out tomorrow," Jasper said, leaning back on the sofa.

"Probably not to the mine," I smirked at him.

"Yeah, not the mine."

I SPENT the morning helping Caspian with some of the horses. He had told me how he thought I should get more comfortable with them. We hauled over some food and scooped it into their stalls. He took one of them out and showed me how to brush it. Afterward, we sat on an old wooden bench outside the barn.

"You and Alpha Forest are welcome back anytime," he offered.

"And you guys are always welcome at West Moon as well," I responded.

"I hope we can see each other regularly. At least once or twice a year. We have a whole lifetime to catch up on."

"I would like that very much," I said honestly.

He nodded his head and reached out his hand to help me up.

"So, where are you and the boys off to this afternoon?"

"I'm not sure. Not the mines," I smiled at him.

"Good. I know I seem tough on them, but I want them to be ready," he explained.

"Do you ever spend time with them like this?"

Caspian looked at me and said, "I don't suppose I do much anymore. Everything has been about training them for their roles in the pack."

"Maybe you should spend some time away from that and more getting to know them again. You know, as I do, how much we each change throughout our lives. You see them when they are working, but do you know them away from that?"

Caspian let out a long, heavy breath, "You are wise, my daughter."

"I wouldn't say that," I said, my cheeks turning pink from the compliment.

"Never doubt yourself. I have only begun to get to know you, and I feel like you have already made a mark in our pack and family. I'm excited to see everything you will accomplish with your own family."

I could only smile at him. I had never had a father figure before, and it was very different from my maternal upbringing. Caspian was tough but supportive. He cared profoundly but in a different way. There were fewer hugs and tears and more laughing and hard work—lessons with my hands. I was so grateful to have experienced it, even for only a week. I hoped there would be more of this in the future.

We started walking back to the pack house. Half way, Caspian stopped.

"Dammit," he cursed under his breath.

"What's wrong?" I asked, concerned.

"He's back."

"Who?"

"Callan. He's the banished warrior. His mate didn't want to leave, so she is still here. He comes back every so often but not usually two days in a row," he explained, the frustration heavy in his voice.

"How can she bear to be apart from him?" I asked, surprised.

His eyes found mine, "I honestly don't know. We've never had a situation like this before."

"I wouldn't think most have. Did you ask her if she wanted to be with him?"

"We've asked her a few times, but she is always adamant that she wants to stay," he looked off in the distance. "I'm sorry, but I need to go. Will you be alright getting back on your own?"

"Of course," I assured him.

He began to strip down. I turned my back to give him privacy. After he shifted and took off, I collected his clothes and returned to the pack house. June was standing out front. I passed her his clothes and stood beside her.

"I wish he would just leave already," she mumbled as she stared to the South.

"Would you be able to leave without Caspian?" I asked her.

She looked over at me with a smirk, "I suppose not. I just don't know what to do."

"I can try to talk to his mate?" I offered.

"I don't know if that would do much. She is stuck in her ways," June's brow creased as she thought about the woman.

"Maybe I can suggest they try with another pack."

"You could, but not many would take in a rogue. Even if they do, they would ask why they were banished in the first place. They would check with us, and if they found out that he disrespected another Alpha, it would be hard to become accepted."

"Was it Forest he disrespected?" I asked, looking earnestly at her.

"It was," she said softly, meeting my eyes.

"Did Forest banish him?" I pressed further.

"No. He allowed Caspian to make the choice. We held a trial. The high-ranking wolves were between stripping him of his warrior title and banishment. When they offered the lesser of the two, he lashed out."

"How so?"

"He screamed at them, telling them they *'couldn't do that,'*" she quoted with her hands while shaking her head in disbelief, "He went on about how strong of a warrior he was and that it would be a grave mistake on their part to take it away from him. After he threatened them, they had to banish him."

"Why would he threaten them? He knew what he was up against."

"We're wolves, honey. We are all a little pigheaded. Being stripped of your status could be considered worse than banishment. Our kind thrives in a pack and our placement within it."

"So...many are not warriors or high ranking. Why would it matter that much?" I protested.

"Sometimes I forget that you haven't been brought up our way," she smiled warmly at me. "The wolves who are born as omegas are the lower-ranked wolves. They are not as strong or fast as the high ranks. They need the protection of their pack and are happy to do their part in return for their safety and security.

"Outside of a pack is dangerous for a lone wolf. Rogues start to become more feral without the hierarchy, and they fight each other constantly. They have a hard time adjusting to the human world. There are too many sounds and scents within the cities, so they often roam the wild in their wolf form. The longer you stay a wolf, the stronger that part of you becomes, and the human side starts to slip away. That is why rogues are so dangerous," she gave me a severe look. "They attack without being provoked. They are filled with jealousy of those who live in packs and the lives we live."

"What would happen to his mate if she joined him?" I asked, deeply interested in learning more.

"It depends if they can find somewhere safe to call home. They will be fine if they find a pack that would take them in. I have heard that some make do living around small towns, working and living almost like humans, but it's rare."

"How do they accomplish that?"

"They have to work for it. When they are banished, they have no money. They must start from the ground up, but lacking a pack can still drive them mad. I've heard it feels like you have no direction. You fight within yourself to determine the best way to do simple tasks. And holding a job is nearly impossible unless you are self-employed. Being told what to do by someone less powerful than yourself feeds our primal nature, and we tend to lash out and become aggressive."

"Why banish wolves at all, then?" I asked.

"If we were to allow them to stay, chaos would follow. Banishment keeps those who challenge the Alpha or his decisions from creating doubt within the pack. Without a strong leader, the wolves inside each of us would doubt the Alpha, and many would be pushed to challenge him. The fight is to the death. Packs have fallen from a non-alpha taking over. They don't hold the strength in leadership to run a pack. They become easy targets for rogues and other packs."

"Wait...how would a 'non-alpha' take control of a pack?" I asked.

"It's rare. Usually, if the Alpha doesn't have an heir and has grown too old, someone like a warrior can challenge him. If they win the fight, they become the new Alpha, yet they lack the power behind their position."

"That's why Alphas are succeeded by their own children?"

"Yes. The moon Goddess pairs up her strongest children to lead. Alpha's mates are usually daughters of Alphas or Betas. Occasionally, they have been omegas, but they are typically strong with a high-rank somewhere amongst their ancestors."

A spark of uncertainty about my ability to give Forest an heir churned in my stomach, but I pushed it aside. I didn't want to spoil the moment with my problems.

"What happens when you have multiple sons, like you guys? Will there be a problem between them in the future?" I asked, concerned for my brothers.

She smiled softly at me, "They will be fine. As you've heard, the other boys will be placed in other high-rank positions. Currently, Oscar will be the Beta, and Cain will be the Gamma. As they mature and grow, that may change. They will find their hierarchy, and things will fall into place."

"What about the children of the current Beta and Gamma? Won't they try and rebel against losing their position?"

She chuckled, "They would never challenge a higher-ranking wolf. They will become lead warriors. Occasionally, a pack will take on a Delta or fourth in command, though that usually happens in large packs like your own. You can't change your placement. There have been a few rare situations where a Beta or Gamma has had an Omega child, and they do not automatically receive their parent title. In those cases, the next strongest is promoted through the ranks."

"This is all wild to me. It's such a different world than the one I grew up in. Our elders are our leaders. They tend to be the strongest, but not always. We place them in leadership due to their wisdom instead." I bit my lip as I processed the information June unloaded on me. "Thank you for explaining all of this to me. I feel like I'm constantly learning," I brought my attention back to her.

"We are all constantly learning. I am here if you ever need me. I know the shoes you are filling," she smiled at me.

"Thank you. I appreciate it."

"Anytime..."

I saw Forest out of the side of my vision and turned to him.

I felt June's hand on my arm, pulling my attention back to her, "Before you go, I'm not sure if it will make a difference coming from you, but it wouldn't hurt to try. Callan's mate's name is Abigale. She lives in the blue house down the road."

"I will stop by and see if I can help."

June nodded once at me before looking towards the South, where I assumed Caspian was. I turned back to Forest and walked over to him.

"Everything alright?" He asked as he wrapped his muscular arm around my waist.

"Yeah, that warrior is back. I offered to talk to his mate."

"Be careful if you do. Mates can go a little crazy without their other half," he warned.

"I will," I said as I stood on my toes to peck his cheek.

5

Juniper

I was supposed to meet up with my brothers in an hour, but I thought I should check in with Abigale first. Forest accompanied me but waited at the road as I approached her door. Her house was simply-built. It looked closer to a trailer than a built-in home, but the foundation gave it away. It was a thin, rectangular house with a low-pitched roof. The simple siding had been painted a light blue color. I knocked on the contrasting dark wood door and heard shuffling from the other side before the door opened, revealing a tall brunette wearing tight jeans and a loose flannel shirt.

"Who are you?" she asked sharply.

"I'm sorry to bother you. My name is Luna Juniper."

I made sure to use my title so that she would not be alarmed by an unknown wolf at her doorstep.

"Luna? You're part of the West Moon Pack?"

"I am."

"Then you should get out of here. Your pack is why my mate has been banished," she sneered through her teeth.

"I'm sorry you have been saddled with such a difficult situation. I had hoped I could help you," I offered, even though I questioned whether I should turn and flee from her deadly glare.

She was obviously angry at us, but I truly wished to help her.

"I don't want your help. You've done enough already!" she screamed at me.

I felt strong hands grip my waist from behind and move me backward. The sparks that flooded through me from the exposed slit of skin on my waist told me that it was Forest.

"You will not speak to my Luna that way," he commanded her.

His Alpha aura was radiating off of him, and Abigale bowed her head. Even though he was not her Alpha, the wolf inside her would cower in front of a wolf of his standing. I could feel his rage through the bond. My fingers touched his tensed back, feeling his muscles relax slightly.

"Come on," I urged him. "It's obvious we can't help her."

Forest didn't move for a moment, letting his Alpha aura push her down for a moment, but he finally relented and wrapped his arm around me as we walked back to the road. Once we were far enough away, I stopped and wrapped my arms around his torso. I could still feel the anger pouring off of him.

"It's alright, Forest," I soothed him.

"It's not. No one talks to you that way. I can't believe she yelled at you," he spat out.

"I'm asking you to drop it. She is upset about not being with her mate. We would both feel the same."

He ran his hand down his face and let out a low growl.

"Seriously, Forest. I probably shouldn't have gone. I didn't think it through," I tried harder to placate him.

"It doesn't matter," he fumed, his anger relentless.

"It does. Her mate was banished for disrespecting you. What would happen if another one of the Silver Ridge members were to face the same punishment due to us? I don't want problems with them," I pleaded to him.

He grumbled under his breath but didn't reply. I hoped that he would let it go. I knew that right now, I needed to get him away from her. When we got back to the packhouse, I saw Cain goofing off out front with some of his friends. They were pushing one another and laughing as they chased each other around. I laughed and shook my head at their little game. June came out front and yelled at them to knock it off before spotting us.

"How did it go?" she asked hopeful.

Forest growled low again. June's eyes widened, and she looked me over, concerned.

"I'm so sorry. I didn't think she would react poorly. Tell me what happened?" she said, rushing up and taking my hands.

"She is just missing her mate," I said, trying to downplay the situation.

"She yelled at you and blamed us for her mate's banishment," Forest refused to accept my answer.

I eyed him sternly but could still feel his frustration and tried not to provoke it further.

"She didn't...? Dammit. I apologize on behalf of our pack, Alpha Forest," she spoke diplomatically to him.

"June, we can let it go," I tried to urge them.

She looked over at Forest, who still had a furious look.

"I'm not sure your mate can. Remember what we talked about earlier," she told me. "It could be a sign of weakness if Forest did not deal with it."

I looked back at Forest and realized what I had asked of him. He protected me, but if word got out that he did nothing to someone who had insulted his mate and pack, it could cause a bigger problem. I set my own opinions aside and let Forest make his grievance against her.

"Let's take this inside to Caspian's office," June suggested, looking between us.

We followed her in as she knocked heavily on Caspian's door.

"Come in," he called out from within.

June led us in to find Caspian at work at his desk. His warm eyes took in June before lowering his pen.

"We have a situation," she informed him.

"What is it?" He asked seriously. They knew each other well enough to know when something was wrong.

"Abigale," She replied exhaustedly.

"What happened with her?" He sat straighter up and squeezed his hands together in front of him.

"Juniper asked if she could talk to her and see if she could help. I told her she could try and told her where to find Abigale. Juniper, why don't you pick up from here."

I chewed on my lip, still struggling with the idea of incriminating Abigale, but I decided that honesty would be best.

"I went to see Abigale. She was not too happy to see me. I told her who I was, and she told me, rather angrily, that our pack was why her mate was banished. I should have left then, but I told her I hoped to help her, and then she screamed at me to leave."

I looked up at my father's reddened face. I held my breath, waiting for him also to discipline my carelessness. Seconds felt like minutes as I waited for him to respond. He looked over at Forest, whose expression was still angry.

"I will handle this, Alpha Forest, if you allow me."

I could see Forest's fists clench, his knuckles white from the pressure.

Caspian spoke again, "Perhaps we shall handle this together."

His eyes clouded over for a second before returning to normal.

"I have called an immediate pack meeting."

WHEN I WENT IN, I found my brothers standing at the front of the dining room. They all smiled quickly as I walked up, Forest close behind me.

"Do you know what this is about?" Cain asked.

Oliver pushed his shoulder, "Quiet. We will find out in a minute."

I was worried the pack would be angry at me for getting involved with Abigale. I watched as they filed in and grabbed chairs from the side, placing them in rows as they sat. Once everyone was seated, Caspian and June walked through the doors and stood at the front of the room.

"I have never been as embarrassed as I have been over these last several months," Caspian started, his voice thick with an angry authority. "Twice now, my pack members have insulted the high-ranks of another pack. Do we not teach you our ways? Have I failed you as an Alpha? If so, today will be my reckoning."

I could see the heads of every pack member in attendance bow to their Alpha. I could feel my father's alpha aura sweep over the room.

"If you are ever visiting another pack or have a pack visiting us, you will treat them with the utmost respect. You will treat them as you would treat your own high-ranks. You do not argue with them. You do not shout and yell at them, no matter what your personal feelings are. You can only disrespect another high-rank if we are at war with them, and we are not at war."

He let out a low growl before taking a minute to calm himself down.

"Perhaps I have been too soft on how I deal with you. I have allowed each of you to stake your claim of innocence before us. Today that will not be happening. Abigale Ellwood, approach your Alpha."

Abigale stood from the back of the room and walked up the aisle to the front, her head bowed low.

"Abigale Ellwood, you have insulted and yelled at a visiting high rank. You have chosen to stay in our pack, knowing the pain of losing your mate. You have chosen to stay and abide by our rules. You have chosen to bear your pain. It is not the West Moon Pack that has caused that. Your mate was banished for his actions, not theirs. You are hereby banished from our pack. Leave now," Caspian said with disdain in his voice.

Her head popped up, meeting his eyes, "please, no! I don't want to be a rogue."

"You have made your choice," he stated definitively.

She lowered her head back down and began to sob. Her shoulders shook from her cries. The rest of the pack started to lift their heads with concern. Their eyes darted towards the windows. I looked over at Caspian, unsure of what was happening.

"Attack!" Caspian called before he looked at us, "rogues, at least fifteen."

We looked back at Abigale, whose cries had morphed into deep, maniacal laughter. She lifted her head, revealing a sinister smirk. Her eyes bore into us with a deadliness.

"Patrols were at a minimum for the meeting," Jasper spoke in realization.

"You," Caspian pointed at her.

"Callan warned you. You should have never underestimated him," she laughed maniacally.

"Grab her!" Caspian ordered.

Before anyone could reach Abigale, she dove towards Forest and me, shifting with her jump. Forest pulled me away as Caspian shifted, his jaws catching her within his hold only inches from where we stood. A sharp crack echoed as he snapped her neck, her lifeless body falling from his mouth. A loud, mournful howl came from the distance.

Callan...

I couldn't believe what had happened in front of us. People were darting all around as they responded to the attack. Chairs were scattered across the floor in a tangled mess, and people shouted commands. Jasper and Oliver had shifted and, along with their father, took off out of the pack house.

"This way," June grabbed my arm and pulled me to the side.

"We're going to help," Forest told me. "Stay with June."

He kissed my forehead before shifting and racing after the others. I looked back at June, who had Cain by her side. She was ushering everyone farther inside the pack house.

"Help me, Juniper," she called to me.

I finally snapped out of my trance and started running towards her. I saw a child huddling under the chairs, so I pushed them out of the way and picked up the small girl. We ran down the hall as June closed a heavy set of wooden doors, sealing us off from the outside.

A woman raced up to me, yelling for the little girl, "Ivy. Ivy, I was so worried! Thank you, Luna."

I passed her the girl and looked around. June was shouting commands to the people who had gathered. I ran up to her.

"What do you need from me?" I asked quickly.

"We need to keep everyone calm."

I looked around the room, assessing the situation. Children were crying as their mothers attempted to soothe them. Others were huddled together, looking worried. I went to the closest group of people to where we were.

"How are you doing?" I asked them sympathetically.

They looked up at me with concern and forced a smile. "We're fine, thank you, Luna Juniper."

I forced a smile and moved to the next group. I continued checking on people until June stood on a chair and called an all-clear. She comforted her pack while they hesitantly began filtering out of the hallways. She eventually approached me, took my hand in hers, and led us to Caspian's office. She closed the door behind us, leaning against it, and deeply breathed.

"Are you okay?" I asked, concerned for her.

"I'm alright," she sighed out.

"What just happened?"

My mind was racing as it tried to combine all the pieces.

"I don't know for sure, but I think we know the real reason why Abigale chose to stay in the pack."

"You mean...?"

"Yes. I think they planned this," she seethed.

"How would they have even been able to recruit the rogues?"

"Rogues are easy to deceive. All Callan would have to do was promise them a place within a pack or even supplies. Some would have even been happy to attack a pack for nothing," she explained.

"Did...did I do this?" I asked, scared that I had brought this on today.

"Absolutely not. Everything that has happened was because of Callan and Abigale. I never would have thought she would have gone to such lengths, but she was always strong-willed. They most likely have been planning this for a long time, just waiting for an opportunity to attack."

"But why go after my dad like that? Wouldn't it be a death sentence?"

"It could have been a last resort. She must have known what would happen after she spoke so callously to you and the meeting was announced. Accounting for the timing of the rogue attack, she must have alerted them. I'm not sure if she was supposed to attack or if she was taking advantage of the situation. Wolves are reactive. Her wolf could have pushed her into it since Caspian threatened her. We will never know for certain. We can only deal with the repercussions."

I felt terrible that I had played into their plan. June held my hand and offered an unspoken comfort. We finally took a seat, waiting for our mates to return. Almost an hour after the all-clear had been called, Caspian and Forest joined us in the office. Caspian walked over to a cupboard and pulled out several glasses, pouring each of us a drink. Beta Leo, Caspian's second, and his Gamma came in after them.

"What happened?" June asked, breaking the silence.

"Callan led a rogue attack on us. It was well planned out. They knew that our patrols were minimized."

A knock came on the door before Jasper and Oliver entered. They stood against the wall.

"How did they know that would happen?" I asked.

"We assume that Abigale told them about the meeting. They were most likely waiting for an opportunity, and we gave them one," Caspian replied cooly, but his anger still ran underneath.

"Were you able to get to Callan?" June asked him.

"No. That coward tucked tail and ran when our warriors arrived. He left the rest of the rogues to fend for themselves. We were able to take down ten of them, and the rest ran off."

"And our warriors?" June inquired.

"They skipped our patrol. The ones who found them are roughed up and will be in the clinic for a while, but they should survive."

"Perhaps I can help?" I offered.

"No," Caspian said adamantly.

He looked at me, deeply understanding what I had offered. I nodded my head in understanding.

"Do you want us to stay and help?" Forest offered.

"I appreciate the offer but don't expect him to return soon. He has been gone for five months and has only attacked now with fifteen. He will most likely try again, but we have time."

"If things change, give us a call."

We each sipped on our drinks as they hashed out what

happened and how to rectify their weaknesses. Caspian had also declared that he wanted each member to attend training on protocols for visiting packs and how to treat other shifters. Both high rank and not. Even though it was evident that Abigale had only stayed to help her mate seek revenge, he would not tolerate her behavior from anyone.

We finally concluded the meeting when dinner time was called. The dining room was quiet as the pack members reflected on the day. I felt sympathy for them and what they had gone through and felt a sadness that we were to leave in the morning after the whole ordeal. I had even missed out on my time with my brothers.

6

Juniper

We stood before the Silver Ridge pack house and said goodbye to my family. I hugged June tightly, finding comfort in her motherly touch. She swept the hair out of my face as we pulled apart.

"Anything you need, just call me," she said, still holding my hands.

"I will," I smiled back at her.

My brothers were lined up to her side. I walked in front of them.

"We will plan to take you out next time you come," Cain half smiled at me.

"I'll hold you to it. Maybe the parents will let you guys visit me sometime. There are no mines, but we have some good hiking trails I can take you up," I offered.

Cain laughed as he leaned in to hug me, "I'm all about that."

I laughed with him. He was always wild and happy, and

his enthusiasm for life was infectious. Next, I looked over at Oliver, who was rolling his eyes at his brother.

"What about you? Maybe someday you will come for a visit?" I asked him.

He smirked before giving me his usual silent nod before smiling. I leaned in and hugged him before moving on to Jasper.

"Thank you for everything," I told him honestly.

"Eh, it's what brothers do, right?" he said indifferently, but the teasing of a smile sat at the corner of his lips.

"Yeah," I snickered at him. "It is. You better convince your dad to let you off the hook for a few days and come and see me. You can call it..." I looked upwards, thinking, "political studies."

He chuckled, "Good idea."

I hugged him and said goodbye to the three of them. It was strange having a sibling connection. I always felt that Meadow had been like a sister to me, but watching her effortless relationship with her sisters always left me wanting more. I never realized how much I wanted it until I felt the bond with my brothers.

My father stood near the car, holding the door open for me. I walked up to him and pushed some dirt with my foot.

"Thank you for having us. It was really nice to come out and see your pack and your family."

"They're your family too, Juniper. Don't forget that," he said softly yet seriously.

"I won't. Thanks, Dad," I said as I hugged him.

I could feel him tighten his hold over me and kiss the top of my head. Finding him seemed to bring so many things into place. I learned all about this other side of me, and I finally knew who my dad was. I wished all of my coven sisters could have a reunion like mine to meet their own fathers.

I stepped back and waved goodbye once more before climbing into the car. I watched as they disappeared behind us. Once they were out of sight, I turned and looked forward as Forest reached over and held my hand. I was sure he felt my sadness at leaving them.

The flight home was no better than the flight there. I still hated being trapped inside an airplane. It felt suffocating, and the noise drove my wolf wild inside me. When we went back onto West Moon lands, much of the pack had come out to welcome us home.

"About time you guys returned. It's so boring here without you," Oakley, our Beta, complained as we walked into the pack house.

I stood in the foyer and looked around at the emptiness. I loved how full and lively the Silver Ridge pack house had been. It reminded me more of my family's home at the coven, just with a few more people. Forest stopped behind me and raised an eyebrow.

"What are you thinking?"

"I think we need more pack meals. It was good to see everyone's faces each day," I told him.

He laughed, "You know we are nearly ten times the size of the Silver Ridge Pack. Where would we fit all of them?"

I pursed my lips at his obvious statement. We would need to build a dining room to fit nearly a thousand people for pack meals. What would happen to the diner? Perhaps we could have both.

"How big do you need to make a dining hall for every-one?" I asked him.

Oakley, who had joined us in the foyer, dropped his mouth open, "You can't be serious?"

"How much space, Oakley?" Forest directed at him.

"Hell, I don't know...around twenty thousand square feet?"

"How big is the community hall?" I asked him.

The community hall was our gathering place for meetings and pack events. Sometimes, it was used for training or sports but often left empty.

"Half of that," Oakley answered.

"You mean it's only ten thousand square feet?" I asked disappointedly.

"Yeah," Oakley said.

I felt defeated. It was the only building large enough to hold the entire pack, but there was no way to make it work unless we wanted everyone to eat with their plates in their laps.

"How old is the building?" Forest inquired further.

Oakley scratched his head as he thought, "Forty, maybe fifty years old."

"Perhaps it's time to build a new community hall," he suggested.

I looked over at Forest, excitement filling me.

"Really?" I asked him.

"Yeah. It has had some problems, and the pack is growing. We could use a new building. One that has all of the modern advances."

"A better HVAC system and new plumbing," Oakley started.

"And room for everyone to dine together if they want," I added.

"We will make it a true community building with a place for the pack to gather."

"A place for the teenagers and kids, maybe even a daycare to help the families with little ones."

August walked in and looked at our excited faces.

"What did I just walk into?" he asked, setting his bag at his feet.

"I have a project for you, August," Forest told him.

WITH SPRING IN FULL EFFECT, I had been busy helping to get the gardens up and running. I knelt down, planting rows upon rows of lettuce seeds. We would plant them in succession for a continuous crop over the summer. I heard heavy footsteps approaching behind me, but I already knew it was Forest. I could always tell when he was near, feeling a magnetic pull to him. I finished with the last few seeds in the row and stood up, brushing my hands off.

"Hey, what are you doing out this way?"

He brushed some dirt off of my cheek with his thumb.

"The plans have been drawn up for the community center, and I thought you would want to take a look."

"You could have linked me instead of coming all this way," I smiled at him.

"And miss out on the opportunity to walk with you?" he replied, leaning in and kissing me lightly.

We held hands as we walked up Main Street towards the pack house. It was the same bustling business that it was every day. The businesses were open, and people gathered at the diner for lunch. Each person bowed their head in respect as we passed them. Once we had made our way to the drive, Forest started telling me more about the community center.

"I think you're going to love what they have come up with."

"You've already seen it?"

"Just a glance."

As we walked down the hallway to Forest's office, August, Oakley, and Lark, an architect in the pack, were waiting outside our arrival. They followed us in as we entered the office. Lark unrolled the plans on the desk, and we all stood around and looked them over. I was mesmerized by the drawings. There was a large room capable of seating up to twelve hundred people for meals. There was a small stage on the side of the room used for meetings and performances by the school children, along with a commercial-grade kitchen that would allow all the food to be made in-house. There were several rooms for the teens and children to gather in, and a daycare was off to one side, with a playground in a fenced area outside of an exterior door. There were several meeting rooms for people to gather and even an indoor basketball court.

We had debated adding a gym but decided that since there was already one at the training facility, we would rather use that area for more gathering spaces. We included a small cafe so those who gathered there during the day could find food and drinks when meals were not being served. This facility also opened up numerous jobs to our pack, which was needed as more of the youth came of age.

"This was a good move," Forest said, kissing my head.

"I think so too. How long will it take to complete?"

"We will need to train a few pack members on construction, but it's fairly straightforward. I would say six months to a year, depending on how long it takes us to acquire the materials," Lark answered.

"If we could try for six months, I think it would benefit the pack greatly over winter," I told him.

"Yes, Luna. I'll start getting some calls in to get the materials shipped."

"Let us know when the delivery trucks will arrive," Forest told him.

"Yes, Alpha."

As Lark rolled up the paper, I asked him, "Is there any way to get artistic drawings of what it will look like?"

"Of course, Luna. My mate is a wonderful artist. I can ask her to draw something up."

"Great, thank you, Lark," I told him excitedly.

"It's an honor, Luna," he bowed his head before leaving.

"What do you want the drawing for?" Forest asked as the others left us.

"I thought it would be fun to share it with the pack."

"Always thinking of the big picture," he said, his adoration for me heavy in his gaze.

I smirked at him before sitting in his lap, "What about building permits? Don't you need those?"

"Did you guys pull permits for your homes at the settlement?"

"On occasion, but we tried to avoid it."

"We are our own municipality, so we just have to file the paperwork to ourselves."

"Really?" I asked, looking at him surprised.

"Yeah," he laughed. "You know that we are a town."

"I know, I just always thought that you still had to file stuff with the territory."

"We file what we need to, but having our own government makes it much easier."

"So, who does the territory think you are?"

"I'm the mayor," he said matter-of-factly.

I folded over myself in a fit of laughter.

"What's so funny?" He smiled at me.

"You have it all figured out, don't you?"

He shrugged his shoulders.

"We've been at this a long time."

7

Juniper

The pack was thrilled at the announcement of the new community center. I could see the enthusiasm on their faces as we went over the details of the new building. Quite a few people had already stepped up to help build it. The first stage was the demolition of our current community center. Since we were in a small valley, space was precious and the ground had already been leveled. They had started a few days after the announcement. Trucks had been rented to help haul away whatever debris we couldn't recycle in-house.

With our pack thriving and growing I decided it was time for a visit to my coven. It had been three months since I had been down there. I had been attempting to alternate the full moons between the pack and the coven, but I had been unable to keep up with it due to my responsibilities within the pack.

Forest drove use down, still refusing for me to go on my

own after last winter's nightmare. A wendigo had attacked my coven while I had been there and Forest and the warriors had to come help us defeat it. Four people had been lost in the battles including Meadow's mother, Heather. This would also be my first time visiting since Meadow and I had our falling out.

Gran had questioned me several times trying to get to the bottom of why we were no longer talking, but I wouldn't dare speak about it. I was concerned what would happen to Meadow if the coven knew she had wanted to leave. I already knew that they would never allow her to come visit me again if the truth were to come out. I hoped that once we mended our relationship, she would be able to come see me again.

We pulled down the narrow dirt drive and stopped in the parking area. The women of my coven began pouring down the trail as they did every time we visited. I was quick to jump out of the car to greet them. We arrived a few days before the full moon so that I could spend time with my family. My Gran stood at the top of the trail holding her fists to her chest with joy.

"Gran," I called to her as I approached.

"Oh, my sweet child. Welcome home."

She hugged me tightly before looking me over.

"Just as I left you," she smiled brightly at me.

"It's good to be here," I told her.

"It is indeed. Hello Forest," she said to him as he followed me up the trail.

"Hello Magnolia."

"Now come, come. I spruced up your home for you."

"You mean my mother's home?"

She squeezed my hand in hers, "I mean yours."

We said our hellos to those we passed as Gran led us through the settlement, across the small bridge and up the trail, passing the Nary house. Quaintly tucked into the forest was the small two bedroom home I had lived in until I was three. Flowers bloomed all around the small front porch.

"It's stunning Gran. You fixed up the garden."

"It was about time we brought life back into this place."

We went in to find the same eclectic furniture placed around the room as before. The slightly worn green lawson sofa with the two toned farmhouse coffee table sat in the center of the room, facing the slate grey stoned fireplace. The mixed styled cabinets graced the walls of the kitchen with a small island. A bowl of ripe fruit sat atop it along with a turquoise cylinder vase bursting with wildflowers. The trebled based rectangular dining table with faded spots in the stain was surrounded my a mix match of dining chairs. I found everything about this space comforting. The bright room looked like a breath of fresh air had swept through it.

"What did you do to it?" I asked my Gran.

"Not too much. It was deep cleaned, decluttered and some new light drapes were hung to let in the light."

"It's perfect," I smiled as I looked across the room.

"I also had a larger bed brought in for the two of you. You can thank your mate for that," she winked at him.

Gran walked over to the refrigerator and opened it up pulling out a salad and some sandwiches, placing them on the small kitchen island.

"I was going to make you something more hearty but my role with the elders takes up too much of my time."

"You didn't need to do all of this Gran."

She held my cheek in her hand, "Of course I did dear. I won't have my grand baby coming home hungry."

I chuckled, "Can you stay and eat with us?"

"I don't see why not. I told those old crows that I would be busy while you were here. I don't think they liked it too much, but what are they going to do?"

We took our seats around the small table and filled our plates. Gran had made plenty of food for us, she always remembered how much Forest could eat.

"So tell me what you two have been up to?"

"We are building a new community center for the pack to gather at. After visiting my father's pack I thought that we needed to come together more."

"That's a wonderful idea, Juniper."

"We will even be able to have meals together, the whole pack."

"How many of you are there again?"

"Just shy of one thousand," Forest answered.

"That will be one busy dinner," she spoke before she took a bite of her sandwich.

"What about you? What has been happening at the coven?"

"Oh you know, same old, same old. I've been busy stepping into my elder role. Elowen Heenan has taken her journey last month. She returned just over three weeks ago."

"Any news if she has conceived?"

"Not yet, but she hopes to find out soon."

My own insecurities about having been unable to conceive a child at this point started the spark once more. Forest held my leg under the table, sensing my need for comfort. We had talked several times about having children, but I had found out when I first met my father that it was rare for a shifter to conceive a child with a non-shifter. I had hoped since I was half shifter, it wouldn't be a problem, but we had not been blessed yet and I feared that it would not happen for us. Even if it were to happen, witches in my coven only birthed females. That opened up a larger world of problems if I could not give Forest a male heir. While our daughter would have Alpha blood, men were always given the role of Alpha due to the natural course of men being larger and stronger. I set my thoughts aside, not wanting to dampen my time with my Gran.

"Hopefully we will hear before we leave," I forced a smile at her.

"Fingers crossed," Gran replied. "You need to meet little Scarlet. She is just the cutest little thing."

"I can't wait to see her."

"Meadow and Willow have been a huge help to Wren with her. You should go see all of them."

I knew that she was trying to push Meadow and me together so that we could reconcile but I was worried that she would still not speak to me. After all, she had avoided me every time I had called.

"Yeah, it would be nice to see all of them."

"We can go now. Scarlet should still be up."

"Oh, right now?"

"No time is better than the present," she said as she pushed her chair back and stood up.

"Would you like to come Forest?" She smiled mischievously at him.

"If it would not be an intrusion."

"Of course not."

We walked back out of the house and in just a few minutes we were knocking on Wren's door. Meadow opened the door and looked at us in shock before turning away.

"That's enough of that, Meadow Nary. You come back her and remember your manners," Gran chided her.

She slowly turned back around, "Of course Magnolia. How are you doing?"

"I'm good, dear. Look who has come for a visit."

She pursed her lips into a tight smile, "Hi..."

"Hey, Meadow. It's good to see you," I told her softly.

"Uh huh. Well I was just heading out. I needed to check in on the stock for mom's company."

She slipped on her shoes and squeezed by us. The whole encounter was awkward at best. I could see Gran shake her head at Meadow as she watched her walk away. When we entered we found Willow sitting at the table with a cup of tea.

"Juniper," she called as she quickly stood and came over to hug me.

"Hey Willow. How are you doing?"

"Good, I've just been enjoying my time with my favorite little niece. Wren is just changing her diaper, but she should be out in a minute."

"I can't wait to meet her."

"She definitely has the Nary look."

"Ginger hair?"

"Ginger hair," she laughed.

"I'm sorry Forest, I was so excited to see Juniper I didn't even say hello to you."

"It's no problem. It good to see you Willow," he told her.

It had taken Forest a few visits before he had grown accustomed to not being at the center of everyone's radar. As an Alpha, he was typically gawked at as soon as he entered a room. Even when we were around humans they could tell he must be powerful by the way he held himself and the aura he put off. But here, he was just a man in a woman's world. I think he has come to enjoy the break.

A little coo drew our attention to Wren who carried Scarletout from the hallway.

"Juniper, Forest. I'm so glad you two stopped by," she said as she walked over to us. "And let me introduce you to our newest little Nary sister, Scarlet," she said as she turned her baby towards us.

The small baby with tufts of vibrant red hair and bright lapis blue eyes looked at us as her mother cradled her.

"Aw, Wren, she's beautiful," I told her as I doted on the baby.

"Thank you. She is quite the wonder. Would you like to hold her?"

"Can I?" I asked excitedly.

"Of course."

She carefully passed Scarlet into my arms. I looked down into her eyes and completely fell in love. I could feel happiness coming through the bond and I looked over at Forest who watched me with love in his eyes. I smiled back at him, but felt that reoccurring ache at the lack of our own child.

"You know, after we lost our mom, I wasn't sure how I would do it without her. I'm so lucky to have my sisters throughout all of it and Scarlet has helped fill the void we felt from mom's absence."

Gran wrapped her arm around Wren's shoulder.

"We always have each other," she told them soothingly.

"We do, and of course we can't forget Magnolia here," she smiled at my Gran. "She has come over nearly everyday to help out where she can."

"You know me," Gran said as she pulled her arm back. "I

can't stay away from a baby. They are pure joy and happiness. I still remember when all of you were this small."

"Oh we know," Willow joked. "You keep telling us about it."

Gran smiled and shook her head.

"What about you two?" Willow asked. "Will you be having babies anytime soon?"

"Us? I think when Selene decides to bless us we will have them," I forced a smile with my response.

Little did they know how deep their question cut me. I knew that they didn't mean any harm by it. I could feel Forest's pain from her question come through as well. It was not just me that ached for a child. It was both of us.

"You just need a good fertility spell if you are ready," Gran chimed in. "It's what we do for all of the other girls here."

"Would they even grant me the spell? I thought that the elders usually waited until someone was twenty-five before they would agree."

"I don't think that they could deny you. After all, you are married to a man."

"Mated," I corrected her.

"Same thing. It never hurts to ask," Gran smiled at me.

We enjoyed our time catching up with Wren and Willow, all while playing with little Scarlet. When dinner time rolled around, we all walked up to the Nary house. Gran had a large pot of stew on the stove that she had been cooking all day. She had instructed Fern, one of my cousins to stir it occasionally.

The whole Nary clan sat down to enjoy dinner together, all except Meadow. I hadn't seen her since she left Wren's house earlier in the day. Even with her absence, I made sure to enjoy my time with my family. After all, it was only a few times a year that I was able to be with them.

"So you actually met your father?" Jasmine, another one of my cousins asked as we sat around the table after our meal.

"I did. It was weird at first, but I visited him and met his family. I have three brothers."

"Brothers..." Willow said almost disgusted.

"They were actually really nice. They all welcomed me into their family. We spent a week there."

"Where do they live?"

"In Colorado."

"They're shifters?"

"Yeah. We visited their pack."

"I wonder what it would be like to meet our human fathers. They would probably freak out and run in the opposite direction."

"I don't know. It was a bit of a shock when he first found out. He even had us do a paternity test to prove it."

"Sounds like a man," my Gran huffed.

"How did you find him?" Jasmine asked.

"Good old detective work."

I still had not told my family outside of Gran and the other elders of my communication with Selene. I didn't want them to look at me differently like Elder Pearl had when she first found out. She had thought I was Selene's chosen one, whatever that meant, and prayed to her at being in my presence. It was overwhelming to say the least.

After a series of father jokes, we said our goodnights to my family and walked back up to our house. I took a quick shower before curling up in our new king sized bed. It made the bedroom look tiny in comparison with only a few feet on either side, but it fit Forest's large frame much better.

"I can't imagine my Gran hauling this in here," I told him as I stretched out.

"I had it delivered and built for her."

I rolled over and looked at him in surprise.

"They let them come in here?"

"I don't think they wanted to do it by themselves," he chuckled with his eyes closed.

I looked up at the wood paneled ceiling, my eyes traveling each crevice between the planks and swirling along with the knots.

"Forest...do you think I should do the fertility spell?"

I could feel him roll over and set his eyes on me.

"Do you want to do it?"

"I'm just worried that I won't be able to become pregnant on my own. It's been nearly a year and it hasn't happened yet."

"I trust whatever decision you decide on."

I rolled back to my side so that I was facing him.

"What if we can't conceive, even with the spell?"

"We've talked about this before. You are all I need. If we are lucky enough to have a child, it would be great, but it's not necessary."

"Wouldn't you be resentful if I can't give you an heir?"

"Not at all Juniper," he said as he pulled me into his chest. "All I need is you."

I sighed into him as he held me tighter. I heard what he said, but I still worried what would happen. His family had been the Alphas of the West Moon Pack for hundreds of years. What if I was the one who put an end to their line?

What would become of the pack? What would become of us?

8

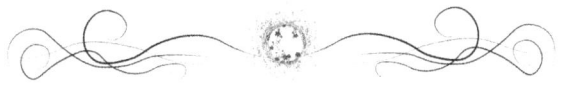

Juniper

I listened to the bird's melodic song above our heads as I led Forest to the meadow. It was one of my favorite spots in the settlement, and I visited it every time I came down to see my family. We passed through a grassy field before entering the towering trees blanketed in moss. The air felt like a mist that held all the secrets of the woods, hiding what was tucked behind each trunk and shrub. I ran my hands across the thick greenery that coated the forest floor. Halfway to the meadow, we crossed a small babbling stream where we used the smoothed stones to walk across. The trees came to a halt, and a large meadow teeming with life graced our vision as the warm sun rays hit our faces. Flowers of every color sprouted up between the green stalks of grass while butterflies and busy bees skirted about.

I ran my hand down one of the wildflowers, plucking it from its stem, and brought it to my nose, inhaling deeply. The intense floral scent invaded my senses. Besides my

mate's alluring scent, the captivating smell of wildflowers was
a close second favorite of mine. Growing up, I would spend
hours lying hidden within the meadow's bountiful embrace.

I had volunteered Forest and myself to collect flowers for
the full moon celebration. We needed flowers of every color,
and I knew exactly where to find them. Both Forest and I
held two large baskets to hold our gatherings. I pulled a pair
of pruners from my satchel and handed them to Forest
before pulling out a second pair for myself.

"Cut at an angle about an inch away from the main
stock," I instructed him.

I watched as he leaned down where he was and went to
work harvesting, and I skipped across the field to the far
side. The lupine and balsam roots preferred the north side
of the meadow, and I wanted to collect as much as possible.
When I spotted the towering light blue flowers, I set my
baskets down and began collecting the stems. My first basket
was filled within a few minutes, so I walked around until I
spotted the balsam root's bright yellow flower. I stepped
from spot to spot, collecting the beautiful blooms.

Glancing over at Forest, I saw that he was still working,
so I lay down amongst the grasses and watched as the clouds
drifted above me, finding pictures and shapes within them.
A cool breeze blew one of my red curls across my face, and I
closed my eyes, savoring the peaceful moment. The warm
sun beat down on my cheeks, warming me until a shadow
blocked its touch. I opened my eyes and found Forest
standing over me, smiling down.

"Did you decide to take a nap?" he asked jokingly.

I took a long breath and smiled back at him, "I thought
about it. It's so beautiful here."

He laid down at my side with his arms behind his head, "It is..."

I returned to watching the cotton-like clouds pass above us.

"Do you see the elephant?" I asked him as I pointed to one of the clouds.

"It looks more like a bear."

"No, it definitely has a trunk," I lightly argued.

He chuckled at my argument.

"That one looks like a wolf howling," he said, pointing to another.

"I can see that. I think you see wolves everywhere," I teased him.

"That actually looks like a wolf, though," he defended.

I laughed, "It does."

His voice was quiet, "Maybe we're supposed to see wolves everywhere."

"It's the wolves in us wishing them into our sight. A way for us to think about them."

"I don't think my wolf needs any help with that."

I rolled onto my side, resting my head on my arm. "It's always good to remember who we are," I said.

Forest pushed himself up and rolled us so that he was hovering above me, looking deeply into my soul. I couldn't help but giggle as he brought his nose down to my neck and inhaled my scent before placing soft, feather-like kisses on my skin. I wrapped my arms around his neck and leaned my head back, arching myself into him.

"You smell so sweet," he hummed out.

"Perhaps you should lick me to see if I taste sweet too?" I urged him on.

I could feel him chuckle in my arms as his warm tongue grazed down my neck. Goosebumps spread from his touch.

"Yup," he said, smiling. "You taste sweet, too. Perhaps I need to investigate further?"

He moved his body down, peppering my skin with kisses and small nips. He pulled my skirt up to my waist before kissing up the inside of my thighs. My breathing deepened as my desire flourished. He pushed my underwear to the side and ran his tongue between my folds with one long sweep before he swirled it around my clit. I lifted my hips in response to the overwhelming sensation, but he anchored them down with his firm, callused hands. He savored me, taking his time. I moaned out and ran my hands through his thick, dark hair, grabbing tight as he built me up. Just as I peaked, he pushed two fingers into me, causing me to unravel. I screamed his name as I threw my head back into the pillow of grass. I panted out my breath as he leaned back to watch me.

"You're gorgeous," he told me. "Your skin is so soft, your lips so sultry."

I smiled as I regained my composure, pulling myself up and straddling his firm thighs. I unbuckled his belt, never taking my eyes off his dark brown orbs. Once I undid his pants, I pulled his length free and slid slowly down on it, groaning in pleasure as I felt myself stretch around him. I rocked back and forth, feeling him glide within me. He held my hips tightly, keeping my movements going even through the ecstasy I felt. I felt my muscles tighten, begging for relief as I cusped my release.

My nails dug deeply into his shoulder as my orgasm spasmed throughout my body, sparks flooding my senses as if a lightning storm had manifested within me. As I came down, my muscles relaxed, giving me more control, but Forest continued our momentum. Moving me with his hands, he kissed one of my breasts and kneaded the other. His tongue flicked my nipple, making me moan. I rolled my head back as he began to build me up again. Both of us panted as I felt him swell within me. With the first burst of his seed, my body clenched down on his, matching his euphoric release.

Our foreheads leaned against one another. Even after all of this time, everything about him drove me wild. I had a hard time pulling away from his toned, broad chest, alluring brown eyes, and his chiseled jaw... even after we just finished our escapade in the flowering meadow. I craved more... more of him. I looked at him with lustful eyes, and he ran his tongue over his teeth as he took in my expression. He leaned forward and kissed me passionately. He rolled us over so that he hovered above me again and began moving with me. I bit my lip and smiled as he caved into my needs.

"Juniper," we heard a call from across the meadow.

We both froze, a look of panic filling my eyes. Luckily, the tall grass would hide us from sight, but I still did not want one of my coven sisters to find us in our throes of passion. I pushed Forest to the side and straightened my skirt while pulling my shirt back down as I heard my name called out again. Forest had tucked himself away and closed his pants. I popped up and looked towards the trail, where I found Willow looking around.

"Hey," I called over to her as I stood up.

When Forest sat up behind me, Willow smirked knowingly. It felt like a walk of shame as we crossed the field to her. At least the baskets of flowers gave us some form of alibi. After all, it was why we had come out here.

"Your Gran sent me to find you," she said mischievously. "She wanted you to come help build the centerpieces for the celebration."

"Uh huh, sure. I will head that way now," I stuttered out.

Willow chuckled as she turned around and walked back down the trail to the settlement. Forest grinned at me before picking up his two baskets, and we started after Willow.

AFTER CREATING centerpieces full of fresh flowers, sprigs of mint, and dried cinnamon, my Gran and I walked back to the Nary house together.

"What really happened with you and Meadow?" She asked when we had freed ourselves from the rest of the group.

"Gran, it's not my place to share," I told her.

She gave me a severe stare down, "If it concerns you, it is."

"Gran, I don't want to talk about it. We had a disagreement. You're the one who told me to be patient with her, and that's what I'm doing," I replied exhaustedly.

"What was your disagreement about? You should share this with me; maybe I can help. I will also remind you that we don't hide secrets in our family."

I was frustrated that she wouldn't let the subject go. Her comment sparked something that had been eating me away over the last year.

I cut her off, "If we don't keep secrets, why have you never told me what happened to the man who killed my mother?"

Last year, when Wren asked to go to Bellingham in hopes of conceiving a child, my Gran protested. It was the same city my mother had been raped and murdered in. My aunt Violet and Gran had words at the meeting. Violet had mentioned that they had taken care of him. I had always wondered what they meant, but I hadn't found a good time to bring it back up to my Gran.

She looked at me stunned, her eyes wide.

She nodded once, "Come, we cannot discuss it here."

She continued walking up the trail but bypassed that Nary house and continued to my home. When we entered, Forest lounged back on the sofa with a book reading. He looked up at us as we walked in, noticing our demeanors. He stood up, placing his book on the coffee table.

"Maybe I'll take a walk," he said quickly before heading towards the door.

"No," Gran said, grabbing his arm to stop him. "I know Juniper will share this with you anyway. You might as well stay."

He nodded his head, and we all sat around the dining table. I could feel my palms start to sweat from the anticipation. Forest placed his hand on my thigh under the table, calming my growing anxiety. We waited anxiously for her to begin.

She took a long, steady breath in, pinching her eyes closed before looking at me full of emotion, "I have told you the story of what happened to your mother."

"Yes."

"I told you how the authorities found him and prosecuted him. He was sentenced to twenty-five years. It pained me to think of him being released and living a life afterward. He had a wife who stood by his side throughout the whole trial. She continued to refuse that he was capable of such atrocities, even with all of the evidence against him."

She paused momentarily, collecting herself before continuing, "He had filed an appeal, and the state was taking another look at his case. I was a wreck, fearful that they would release him. His wife was advocating for him on the outside. I went to see the elders, begging for their help. Even they knew that Selene would not be happy with someone who had killed one of her children being released. The elders and I cast a bad luck spell upon him, hoping his appeal would not be approved. When his wife found a capable lawyer who obviously had no qualms with allowing a murderer back onto the streets, he sent a barrage of filings to the state; I knew that our spell had not done what I had hoped."

Her eyes locked with mine, and I could tell she was holding her breath. My throat constricted, and it felt like the world around us stood still, waiting to hear what she would say next.

"I cast a hex on him," she confessed.

My mouth dropped, and I stared at her in disbelief.

"Gran! We are light witches. We're never supposed to dabble, let alone cast in the dark arts," I nearly shouted.

"I know," she looked down at her hands. "I just couldn't bear thinking he would walk free."

"What did you hex him with?"

"Poor health. I had hoped that if he were too unhealthy, perhaps he wouldn't be able to stand trial again. I hadn't realized that he already had health problems, and paired with the bad luck spell, he had a heart attack. He died the day after I cast it."

"Gran..." I whispered, but she held up her hand, stopping me.

Her face hardened, and she continued, "Violet figured it out. After I had cast the hex and we heard word of his death, she came to me. She could sense the change in my power. She performed a cleansing ritual, telling the rest of the coven that I needed space after all that had happened. She hid me out in the woods, where she cleansed me every day for two weeks until all of the darkness had been cleared from me."

I was speechless. Our coven could use spells to protect ourselves, but she had actively cursed a man. Even him being as evil and heartless as he was, it went against all of our beliefs. There were dark witches out there. They gained their power from the darkness rather than the light. It consumed them. They often traveled the world alone, cursing anyone who stood in their way. The only reason they kept themselves hidden was so that they were not hunted down.

I reached over to Gran and held her hands tightly in mine.

"Thank you for sharing with me," I whispered to her.

She wiped a lone tear from her eye and looked up at me, "I have been honest with you. I expect that you will be honest with me as well."

I had hoped she would have forgotten about Meadow and me with her confession. Now I had to tell her. I could not keep it hidden any longer. I sighed and pulled my hands back.

"Meadow thrived at our pack. When the day came for her to return," I paused for a moment, "she didn't want to leave.

She said she wanted a family, a life outside of the coven. I told her that if she left the coven, then I wouldn't be able to allow her to stay with the pack. She asked me to leave, too, but I refused. I don't want to give up the coven. To give you up. She accused me of having everything and that the rest of you had to live within the restrictions of the coven. She would never be able to fall in love. She has refused to talk to me since."

"Oh, Juniper. That must have been very difficult. Why have you not shared this with me sooner?"

"I didn't want her to be punished for wanting to leave. Even if she weren't, I didn't think the coven would ever allow her to return to revisit me once they found out about her struggles. I love her, and I loved having her there."

Gran held my cheek softly with her hand, "She is lost and confused. She has had a difficult year filled with many losses. You did the right thing, but I understand the difficulty. We can only hope that Selene will guide her through it."

I nodded and leaned into her hand. I felt like a weight had been lifted from my shoulders after sharing with Gran. Looking into her eyes, I knew she would not hold it over Meadow or tell the rest of the coven. Just as she has kept her own secret all these years, she would keep my words close to her heart. Perhaps now she would be able to help Meadow.

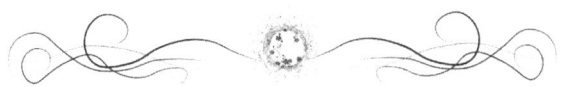

9

Juniper

I pulled my long black cloak over my shoulders, tying the satin ribbon around my neck. Forest watched me as he leaned on the doorway. He wore a sleek black button-down shirt with black slacks. Having been to several of our full moon celebrations over the last year, he knew what to expect and how to dress. He was always good at staying in the background, allowing us to perform our rituals while maintaining his protective presence. Even with a swarm of naked women in front of him, he kept his sight on either me alone or off towards the woods, respecting each of the other women.

"Are you ready?" he asked as his eyes ran up my body.

"I am. Let's go."

We walked down the darkened trail. Night had grasped the forest around us. I was thankful for my wolf's enhanced eyesight, which allowed us to see with pristine clarity even without using lanterns to find our way. The light of the settlement and the raging bonfire at its core grew as we walked closer. I could hear the laughter of others echo up the trail, signaling that the festivities had already begun. I found my Gran and several other Nary women sitting at one of the rustic wooden tables that circled the bonfire and walked over to join them.

"The glorious flower moon," Willow said as she sat at the table with a plate piled with food.

"It is a powerful one," Gran smiled at her. "You know tonight allows for our most powerful of spells, so if you have anything you're hoping to fulfill this year, now is the time."

I saw her looking over at me with a knowing twinkle in her eye. I wasn't sure what she was implying unless she was referring to the fertility spell. I intended to ask her, but before I could say anything, Wren walked up, handing Scarlet over to her sister.

She blew out a breath and straightened her hair as she said, "I'm starving. Would you mind holding her for a moment?"

"Not at all. I love this little *binneas*," Gran cooed over Scarlet.

Forest walked over, setting a plate piled high with food before me. A heavy harvest of peas, along with some other salads and venison, filled the plate. The inviting smell of roasted herbs and meat made me salivate. I licked my lips excitedly as I grabbed my fork and dove in. Wren returned with her own plate of food, setting it on the table before pulling her daughter into her lap.

"I can hold her while you eat, dear," my Gran offered.

"Thank you, Aunt Magnolia," Wren replied with heavy appreciation as she passed the baby over.

"Where is Meadow?" Gran asked Wren.

"I'm not sure," she replied, looking around the gathering area for her. "I thought she would have already been here. Maybe she was held up by something."

I knew why she wasn't sitting at our table as she was every other full moon. She was stubborn and had decided avoiding me was the best thing to do. We finished our meals and sipped on our mint juleps while waiting for the ceremony. I finally caught sight of Meadow right as Elder Pearl began to gather everyone around the bonfire. We each took our place, side by side, shoulder to shoulder, as Pearl stepped forward and began to chant.

"*Ath-bhreith, torachas, seusan ùr oirnn. Bidh sinn a' tabhann na flùraichean dhut agus ar cridheachan Selene.*" her voice echoed across the clearing.

Her cloak dropped off her eighty-two-year-old frame, though anyone other than a sister of the coven would have a hard time believing her age. Our coven's youthful look was all thanks to our light magic. One by one, each sister dropped their robes to the ground, baring themselves to Selene and the power of her moon as they repeated Pearl's chant. I held the hands of the women around me as we began to dance around the circle, skipping and laughing. I could feel Selene's power flowing into me, making me feel alive and energetic. Drinks were passed out, and the circle split as the women danced to their own steps. Several women picked up instruments that had been placed to the side and began to play.

I skipped over to Forest, grabbing his hands and pulling him with me. My arms wrapped around his neck as we swayed side to side. Though the music was lively, I couldn't help myself but become entranced with his eyes, only hearing the beat of his heart.

"Thank you for coming with me," I whispered to him.

"I always want you to be happy, Juniper."

I kissed him lightly, savoring my moment with him.

"Come on, you two love birds, dance with us," Willow called from the side.

I leaned my head on his chest and smiled at her.

"You go have fun with your coven. I'm going to go for a run," he whispered into my hair.

I looked at him and ran my hand down his stubbled cheek. "I'll meet you afterward."

"I'll be waiting," he said, nipping my ear before turning away.

I suddenly felt cold and empty without him, but I knew that my coven was more comfortable this way. I watched him disappear into the darkness before turning back to find Willow. She had gone over to dance with Meadow and Wren. I approached, hoping that Meadow would not flee.

"Hi, Meadow," I said to her.

"I think I'm going to go grab another drink," she said in an annoyed whisper to her sisters.

We watched as she disappeared amongst the others.

"That sister of mine has such a stick up her ass lately. What happened up at your pack?" asked Willow.

"I think she's mad that I get to live in two worlds."

"She has always loved the outside. She thinks it's always greener than what we have here. Even in the month I spent in Birmingham, I saw how they lived. No one cares for anyone else," Wren said with disdain when she thought of her journey.

I nodded knowingly but also dared not risk exposing the rest of the truth to them.

"Let's not let her dampen the night. She can go sulk on

her own," Willow continued as she grabbed my hand and started dancing.

I had always been closest to Meadow since we were the same age. Willow was six years older than us and had her own friends. I wasn't sure why she was making such an effort with me, but I wouldn't turn down her kindness. I got lost in the music and the festivities as we danced.

The party was still strong, and only a few had retired: Those with younger children needed to put them to bed, while the rest of us would enjoy our time late into the early morning hours. Our celebrations would often go until sunrise, pulling as much of Selene's power within us from the full moon as possible. I guessed it was close to three in the morning when I decided I wanted to find my mate. I snuck away from the celebration and made my way towards the woods. When I was sheltered from view, I allowed my wolf to come forward, shifting into my other form. I stretched out my paws and shook my fur before taking off through the trees.

I could smell a rabbit nearby, and while my wolf wanted to go after it, I steered her back to our task of finding Forest. I assumed he wouldn't have strayed too far, knowing I would be coming to find him eventually. I picked up his scent near the stream and followed it upriver. After ten minutes, the trail disappeared. I searched the area but couldn't figure out where it picked back up.

Where are you? I linked him.

I've been waiting, he replied in a husky voice that sent a shiver of excitement through me.

The wolves inside us craved to hunt, and what was better than chasing down our own mate? It was one of the greatest forms of foreplay. My head darted around, realizing he had set a trap. A light breeze blew past me, carrying his scent. I turned in the direction it had traveled from but couldn't catch sight of him.

I turned and ran as fast as possible, happy to oblige in his little game. I could hear movement behind me as he took chase, but I knew these woods better than him. I darted down the stream, cutting off where the forest thickened. Careful with my footing, I tried to make as little noise as possible as I snuck through the undergrowth. I found a hiding spot near a fallen tree and lay in wait for him, ready to pounce.

Tricky little mate, he teased me.

I think we know who the tricky one is.

I listened for movement but only heard the usual sounds of the night: mice scurrying, an owl calling overhead, and the breeze rustling through the newly emerged leaves. Where could he be? A slight rustling came from behind me. I already knew he had circled around and snuck up on me. I wasted no time, leaping from my spot and darting forward— a crash of leaves from where I had just been told he had nearly had me. I chuckled as I escaped, fleeing once more through the labyrinth of trees.

His thundering footsteps echoed behind me as we raced through the forest. I broke into the meadow thinking I could hide within the grass, but before I could duck down, I felt my body tumble along with his as we rolled atop the flowers. My wolf yipped in joy at the fun we were having. His wolf licked the sides of my muzzle as we came to a stop.

He shifted back, and I followed his lead. I ran my hands down his taut, muscular arms. We both knew what we wanted. Words were not necessary. He kissed me passionately, pushing his tongue into my mouth. He held the back of my neck, pulling me closer to him. I couldn't wait any longer.

"Forest, I need you now," I moaned out.

He flipped me over so I was on my knees and pushed deeply into me. I screamed out in pleasure as he began pounding into me with such force. I loved every second of it. I could feel him hitting the very back of my core. I quivered beneath him as I nearly instantly peaked. His hand kneaded my breast as his mouth roamed my shoulder. I arched into him, desperate for everything he would give me. I screamed out once more as a symphony of fireworks burst within me. Forest bit into my mark, sending my already euphoric body further into the realms of pleasure. Lights danced in my eyesight as my whole body responded. Every muscle tightened and reveled in the immense pleasure he gave me. As the world returned to me he released his bite, kissing the skin.

He stood up, still impaling me as my hands supported me on the ground. Forest supported my lower half as he continued his thrusting. He reached new depths as he took me with my hands pushing into the earth, and my ass lifted to the heavens. I moaned over and over.

"F-forest," I called out through panted breaths.

"Juniper, you feel so good," he grunted in response.

The cool breeze nipped at my hardened exposed nipples, heightening my senses while his fingers dug into my skin as he anchored me in place. All I could hear was skin slapping skin as he pushed deeper inside of me. I could feel myself build as my body tingled, starting at my core and spreading like wildfire throughout my limbs. I moaned before biting my lip. A scream worked its way up my throat. My body burst with pleasure. I would have collapsed to the ground if not for Forest's firm hold on me. I felt my walls tighten their hold on him as he pulled everything from me.

We would not let up until after the sun's rays began to grace the land. Our bodies stayed tangled in the heat of passion. The only witnesses were the animals that called the forest home. When we finally succumbed to our exhaustion, we fell asleep in each other's arms, surrounded by the matted-down grass around us.

10

Juniper

"Wake up, Juniper," Forest called as he gently shook me awake.

His voice sounded off. As I came to my senses, I could feel his anxiousness. I quickly sat up and looked around, finding nothing but the meadow around us.

"What's wrong?" I quickly asked him.

"We need to leave," he said, his voice far more severe than expected.

"Why?" I asked as concern began to fill me.

"Your father's pack has been attacked."

I jumped up, and we began running down the trail back to the settlement.

"How do you know?"

"Oakley is in town. He drove down to tell us."

My settlement had no cell reception, so the only way to reach us was to call the landlines. There was one in each of the family houses, but if they had called last night, no one would have been home. A feeling of unease settled in the pit of my stomach. The attack must have been serious for Oakley to have driven down to us.

We stopped at the edge of the trees where Forest had left his clothing. He slid on his slacks and gave me his shirt. We rushed through the center of the settlement, finding it empty. Everyone would most likely still be sleeping. Judging by the sun, it was still early morning. Most of the coven would not be waking until closer to midday.

When we arrived at the Nary house, I slipped inside to inform my Gran that we had to leave. Forest continued to our home to collect our belongings. I slipped on one of the robes left near the door so my nude attire wouldn't be startling to anyone inside. I tiptoed up the stairs and came to her door, knocking quietly before cracking it open.

"Gran?" I whispered, calling into the darkened room.

I could hear her even breathing, telling me she was still asleep. I walked over to her bed and gently rubbed her arm. Her eyes fluttered open, and she quickly sat up.

"Juniper, is everything alright?"

"I'm sorry for waking you, but Forest and I must leave. There is an emergency that we have to get back."

"I hope it's nothing serious," she said.

"I'll call you later and let you know."

"At least let me make you a quick breakfast," she offered as she started to pull her blankets off.

"We don't have time, but thank you."

"Okay, dear. Please be careful."

"I will," I smiled back at her.

By the time I walked back out of the front door, Forest was coming back down the path with our bag in hand. He held a dress for me, and I quickly changed, giving no worry about wearing any underwear underneath. He put his shirt back in the bag, and we took off for the car. He drove off quietly, not wanting to wake anyone, but as soon as we reached the main road, he sped off. The nearby town was usually a thirty-minute drive, but he had us there in half that. We pulled up outside of a diner where Oakley was waiting for us. He climbed into the back seat, and we took off once more.

"What happened?" I turned to ask him.

"An army of rogues led by the former Silver Ridge warrior attacked the pack last night. They came while they were on their pack run. They killed their patrols and attacked the pack house."

I gasped and covered my mouth with my hand.

"What about my family?" I asked him, scared to hear his answer.

"Your brother Cain was severely injured. By the time the rest of the pack returned, they had already killed several of the women and elders who had stayed back to watch the pups. The rogues fled when the pack approached."

"We need to go right now," I stared at Forest urgently.

"I sent a group of warriors as soon as the call came in. They should be there around noon today. When we couldn't reach you, I drove down immediately to inform you both," Oakley told us.

"Good," Forest said. "We will head straight to the airport. Have someone pick up your car and ours and return them to the pack."

"Yes, Alpha."

"Get us on the first flight out. I should be able to get us to the airport in two hours," Forest added.

"Yes, Alpha," Oakley replied as he pulled out his phone to make the arrangements.

Forest sped down the highway, flying past other cars.

"Careful, Forest," I told him.

"They attacked the children, Juniper," he seethed.

I could feel his anger boil through the bond. I knew that whatever was to happen, Forest would not let a single one of them live.

WE PULLED onto the Silver Ridge drive, passing under their wooden ranch sign. A handful of men stood near the gate, acting like they were working on some fencing, but I knew that the patrols had been strengthened. Forest rolled down his window as one blocked the way.

"Alpha Forest," one said as he approached. "Alpha Caspian is waiting for you at the pack house."

Forest rolled up his window and sped down the dirt road. I couldn't believe what I saw as we approached the house. What once was a beautiful wood and stone building looked as if it had seen a war. Nearly every window had been smashed out, glass littering the soil beneath. The heavy wood doors that used to be front and centered on the building were laid out on the ground out front, ripped from their hinges. The entire right side of the pack house was black from what looked like a fire. I jumped out of the car as June and my dad came to meet us. I rushed up and hugged my father. He held me tightly for a minute before pulling back.

"Thank you for coming. Your warriors arrived a few hours ago. They are out at our borders."

"Are you sure it was your warrior again? He lost his mate the last time we were here. Surely the break in the bond has taken him," Forest directed the question at Caspian.

"It was without a doubt. We believe that the madness has taken him."

"He was most likely already affected by his feral side when he had been banished. I can only assume that his mate's death pushed him over the edge," Forest mused.

"It may have been what saved his life," Caspian replied.

"What do you mean?" I asked.

"As you know, when we lose our mates, we typically die as half of our soul has been ripped from our body. In such instances, some may survive, but only at the cost of turning feral. Our wolves take over our consciousness, and we lose ourselves to our inner beasts. If he were already teetering on the edge of becoming feral, his wolf would most likely have already had a greater hold on him when his mate died, and that pushed him in that direction instead of his human side collapsing from within. He will forever be stuck in an aggressive mindset. Blood and death will be his only goals in life," Forest answered solemnly.

I could feel my throat tighten from fear. Day by day, I learned more about our kind. Most of it was truly magical, but parts truly scared me. I couldn't imagine my humanity being taken from me completely. Would I even still be me if that were to happen?

"And the injured?" I asked, needing to change the subject.

"We have a small clinic, but it was destroyed in the attack. We have the injured in some of the rooms upstairs, but we have no doctor. Our healers are doing what they can."

"So many children," June cried.

"Show me where," I told her, determined.

I could help. I refused to hide my powers if I could use them to save people. June didn't hesitate as she led me into the pack house. Piles of debris had been swept around the edge of the area. We traveled up the staircase to the first room. Several children sat on mattresses on the floor. They looked bruised, but otherwise, okay. On the bed, I spotted Cain's familiar face. He was unconscious, with bandages wrapped around his head, and his arm was in a sling.

"He tried to fight them off," June told me softly. Her worry for him was like a wet blanket in the room.

I walked over to him and pushed the hair out of his face. I could tell that his injuries were grave. I pulled the blanket down and looked at his abdomen. It was blue and swollen. I looked back to June with worry in my eyes.

"The healers say that he has internal bleeding."

"Why not take him to the hospital?" I asked her.

"His blood is different from a human's. They would be able to tell that he is not one of them. We cannot take him to a hospital without risking exposure," she cried.

"I can heal him, but it needs to be under the moon."

"Please," she begged, kneeling in front of me. "Please save my baby."

I kneeled with her, "I will do everything I can."

Her pain hit my heart, and I wondered if I could perform the beatha gealaich spell during the day. Each time I cast it, it took less of a toll on me. I felt around my neck for my moonstone necklace. Aspen, one of our pack members, gave it to me the first time I performed the spell, and I have kept it with me ever since.

"Is he the worst?" I asked June.

"One of them," a healer said as she entered the room. "There are three others who will most likely not make it. Two mothers and a five-year-old girl."

"Can they make it until tonight?"

"Only the goddess knows," the healer answered.

I could save Cain during the day but could not cast such a powerful spell four times under the sun. There simply wasn't enough power to pull from. Then, an idea came to me. I could try and heal all four of them simultaneously, with one casting, but I would need the power of the moon to do it.

"Show me the others," I said, needing to better assess what would be required.

Forest

I watched Juniper rush into the house after June and returned to Caspian. His face showed a mix of anger and sorrow, two emotions I understood. He had failed to protect the most vulnerable of his pack. The guilt would be eating him from the inside. The only way to help him through it would be to take revenge on those responsible.

"Is there a place we can talk?" I asked him.

"My office, they didn't get into it."

We walked through the damaged building to his office doors. He unlocked them, opening an untouched room. He walked over and poured each of us a drink before sitting across from me.

"They took out the patrols before they could send a warning. We heard The first alarm from one of the women in the pack house. The children were out back playing. They were just about to send everyone home. Callan knew that they would be here unprotected," he started.

He swirled the amber liquid around in his glass as he retold his story.

"The mothers and elders, who were watching the children, saw them come through the trees. They yelled at the children to run inside, but the wolves were faster. They targeted the adults first. This allowed some of the children to hide inside. Cain..." he paused as he collected himself, "he tried to stop them. Without his wolf, he didn't stand a chance. He is strong, and I have trained him to fight, but he was up against many. From what I can tell, they were able to grab ahold of his shoulder and throw him into a tree. We are unsure if he will survive."

"Juniper can help him," I assured him.

He looked up at me with hesitant hope.

"I hope so...After they killed the adults, they forced their way into the house. The children had attempted to lock the doors, but the wolves attacked before they could get them all. The rogues came in and started attacking the children, while others began to destroy the house. They went room by room, doing what damage they could. When we arrived, they took off. We chased them down, killing five along the way. Most were able to escape."

"How many were there?" I asked, stunned.

Rogues typically stuck to themselves. Once in a while, there would be a small group, usually a family or two, but without an Alpha, they were bound to fight each other.

"From what we can tell, around forty."

I sat back in shock. It was unbelievable. The last time the rogues had gathered into a group that size was during the Rogue Wars over twenty years ago.

"I'm not sure what Callan said to recruit them, but it seems to have been a powerful buy-in," he continued.

"We will stop them. None shall live to tell the tale of what has happened here. How many have you lost so far?"

"We lost eleven last night, including two children. I expect we may lose a few more from the mate bond."

"Juniper may be able to help with that as well."

"What do you mean by that?" he asked curiously.

"Last winter, we lost a warrior. His mate withdrew, refusing anyone to be near her. I left Juniper there with her. She wanted to see if she could help. My Beta was there. He told me that they heard a commotion and went racing to them. When they entered the room, the woman was crying and began to speak for the first time since her mate passed. Whatever Juniper did to her helped bring her back. She is still recovering from losing her mate but has rejoined the pack. She cares for her children and goes to work every day."

"I've never heard of such a thing. Even the mates who survive their mate's death usually withdraw from the pack, eventually fleeing to become a rogue."

"Juniper is very powerful," was all I thought to say. "My biggest concern is what will happen if her capabilities are discovered. My pack is under my command never to speak of it to outsiders, but your pack is not."

"Understandable. Whatever she does for us, I will demand the same from my pack," he assured me.

"Thank you."

As the last year passed and more of Juniper's powers revealed themselves, I realized what a target she could become. Shifters of all kinds would want to use her. When a pack member was lost, you lost two due to the mate bond. She could bring us back from the brink of death, healing our

wounds. I had become more protective with each new reve-
lation of her power, but I had not shared this with her. I
didn't want her to become fearful of others, of the world.

Caspian and I began to lay out a plan. We needed to
protect the pack and hunt down the rogues. It had only been
a few weeks since their last attack, but Juniper and I would
not be able to stay that long if they were to wait before
attacking again. Our own pack needed us. We had already
been gone for several days before we came here. The longest
I had been away was three weeks, and I could feel the effects
on my pack when I returned. They needed their leader to
guide them. To be there to help with their problems. August
had stayed back to watch over the pack in our absence, but
that would only be able to last so long before the wolves
inside of them would start to push the boundaries.

With the loss of eleven pack members, nearly a tenth of
their pack had been killed. Another four were in no state to
help after losing their mates.

"How many warriors do you have left?"

"We train all of our men to be warriors. Being a medium-
sized pack, we have needed to follow this thinking in order
to protect ourselves."

"Smart," I told him.

"We have around thirty warriors at the moment, not
including myself and the other high-ranked."

"Forty against forty to begin with. Callan seems to have
planned his attack accordingly."

"I thought that too. Though, he was smart enough to
have them retreat when they did. We both know that pack
wolves are far better trained than rogues."

"Yes. I have brought another fifty warriors with me. They
now face twice the force. We should keep at least half here

when we go in search of them. They will be on standby if needed, but protecting the rest of your pack will be the priority."

"When do we leave?"

"I say first thing in the morning. We should be able to pick up their trail. Forty wolves moving around are sure to leave a sizable mark to follow."

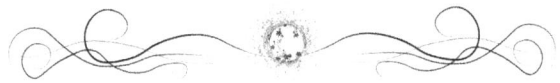

11

Juniper

With the sun having set and the moon taking its place in the sky, I prepared to perform the ritual. June had helped me gather more moonstones. Fortunately, they were a favored gemstone amongst shifters. I could hear my father in the dining room as he began to speak to his pack. I listened in from the next room.

"The West Moon pack has come to help us defeat the rogues that have taken many from us. In addition, they will help our injured. The methods they use are not to be spoken of," he commanded them in his Alpha tone.

Even I could feel the waves of power in his voice. I peeked into the room, finding everyone's heads down in submission from his command. I was not ashamed of what I was, but Forest had told me that it was better if word did not travel about it. Just as the coven stayed hidden, I knew it was the right choice, so I stayed quiet.

"Tonight, you will all stay away from the pack house.

While I know you want to stay here for safety, understand that we have an additional fifty warriors patrolling our borders. The rogues will not pass. If you have a home outside of the pack house, I ask that you go there and open your doors to others who will need a place to stay. It will just be for tonight."

He concluded his meeting and walked out of the room, spotting me.

"How are you feeling, Juniper?" he asked quietly as he approached me.

"I'm fine. They don't need to leave their homes."

"The injured are too critical to move far away, and I do not want to make it a spectacle."

"If you're sure..."

"I am," he said with conviction.

I knew that there was no point in arguing further. Forest walked up behind me and wrapped an arm around my waist as he nodded at my dad.

"I have instructed forty of my warriors to cover the borders along with yours. The remaining ten will be here at the pack house to help protect Juniper."

"Good, we can start in about thirty minutes. I need to give my pack enough time to gather their things," he said before giving us a quick nod and leaving to help his pack make their accommodations.

Forest pulled me to the side into an unused room, "Is this going to be too much for you? I don't want you risking yourself."

I could feel his concern. I wrapped my arms around his neck and looked up into his eyes.

"I need to try. If it becomes too much, I will pass out, but I will be fine," I assured him.

He grumbled at my answer, displeased that I could become unconscious. The spell could wipe not only all of my energy but all of my power. I had refrained from healing the mates of the deceased earlier so that I could store as much power as possible to try and heal the critically injured. The mates would have a few days before becoming too stricken, hopefully giving me enough time to heal. I could return to the waterfall my father had taken me to when we first visited to recharge if needed.

And Cain...I just found my brothers, and in that short amount of time, I had already formed a bond with them. I couldn't lose Cain now. He was full of life. What type of sister would I be if I didn't do everything I could to save him? I had made up my mind the second I saw him lying helpless. His once bright face was pale and void of the life it usually carried. I could feel him slipping away when I touched him. Even the thought of it broke my heart.

"I need you not to freak out," I told Forest.

"I don't know if I can watch my mate give herself completely to others. You're sacrificing yourself for them," he said worriedly.

"Just as you would do for our pack. These are women who fought with their lives to save children, a child of only five, and my brother. You cannot ask me not to do this. You have to have faith that I will succeed. Only with you behind me will I have the strength to do it."

A tear slipped from my eyes. Forest cupped my cheek, brushing it away with his thumb.

"I will be what you need me to be," he said hesitantly.

"Promise?"

He looked deep into my eyes, "I promise."

I stood in the field behind the pack house. We had laid blankets side by side on the four spots where the injured would be placed. Bowls of water sat at the head of each blanket. I watched as the warriors carefully carried each of the injured out, placing them as close as possible. I needed to be able to touch each one. I kneeled down in the center, two on my right and two on my left. I placed a moonstone on each of their chests and looked up at Forest again.

I give you my all, he linked me.

I smiled at him and looked around at the warriors around us. My dad, June, and my other two brothers were there as well, their faces full of pleading hope. I prayed that I wouldn't disappoint them. I had considered performing the spell one at a time but was concerned I would pass out before I could get to all of them. How would I choose who to do first? I had to hope that this would work. Something inside of me said it was the right choice. I had to follow my gut.

I reached across the person on either side of me, my arms pushing down on the moonstones. My hands covered the moonstones on the two furthest away. I stretched out as far as I could to have them all within my reach. I took a long, deep breath and closed my eyes, focusing on my energy, my power. I felt it within and channeled it as I began to chant.

"*Selene, mo mhàthair. Thoir dhomh do sholas gus an urrainn dhomh beatha a thoirt air ais dha do chlann. Cleachd mi mar do làmhan, do shùilean agus do bhodhaig. Thoir do thiodhlacan don leanabh agad. Is ann leatsa a tha mo bhodhaig airson a chleachdadh airson do adhbhar.*"

After the first chant, I could feel the immense pull on my

power. I repeated it a second time, feeling myself drain even more. By the third time, my body struggled to keep my arms stretched out, but I pushed through. I had to fight the fatigue if I wanted to save these people.

"*Selene, mo mhàthair. Thoir dhomh do sholas gus an urrainn dhomh beatha a thoirt air ais dha do chlann. Cleachd mi mar do làmhan, do shùilean agus do bhodhaig. Thoir do thiodhlacan don leanabh agad. Is ann leatsa a tha mo bhodhaig airson a chleachdadh airson do adhbhar,*" I chanted again.

My eyes became heavy, and my voice began to quiver. With the fifth and final chant of the magical words, I felt the darkness overtake me as the last of my energy was pushed into the others. I had nothing left as I collapsed to the ground.

Forest

I KEPT my anxiety at bay as I watched Juniper heal the Silver Ridge injured. I knew how important this was for her. I could quickly tell when the energy began to be pulled from her. I nearly tried to stop her more than once. When she collapsed to the ground, I dropped to my knees. The bond had passed her exhaustion to me, and I felt like I could barely stay awake, but I had to for her.

Caspian rushed to her unconscious body as Silas, one of my warriors, helped me up. June flew over to Cain, dropping to the ground next to him as his eyes began to flutter. I could hear her sobs that she had fought to keep at bay. Silas helped steady me on my feet as June turned to us, tears pouring down her cheeks.

"What's up, mom?" The words came from behind her.

Her head whipped back around as Cain sat up. His confused expression was evident.

"What's going on?" he asked, looking around. The others began to sit up as well.

"Mama," the five-year-old girl said to the woman beside her, "why are we in the field?"

The woman looked around, confused as well, "I don't know, baby." She looked over at Caspian, "Alpha, what's happening?"

Caspian lifted Juniper in his arms. I tried to step forward to take her but stumbled slightly. He looked back at me and shook his head.

"I have her Alpha Forest. She is alive."

"We need to get her to water," I told him.

She had not left instructions on how to help her recover, but I knew that water would be how we could help bring back her energy.

"A bath?" June asked as she held Cain in her arms.

"No, a stream or river would be best."

"Okay, is someone going to tell us what just happened?" Cain asked, pulling away from his mother's tight embrace and standing up.

Jasper walked up to him and pulled him into a tight hug, "She saved you, dumb ass."

Cain watched as Caspian rushed towards the barn. I followed as quickly as I could, my energy slowly returning. The need to protect my mate fuels me.

"Stay with her," I ordered my warriors.

They rushed after Caspian. Silas looked at me for confirmation that he, too, should go. I swept my head in their direction and watched them take off, disappearing into the barn with Caspian. Caspian told my warriors how to saddle their horses when I walked in. Juniper was carefully placed on a blanket in the hay as he jumped on the back of a horse bareback.

"Hand her to me," he barked at Silas.

"I got her," I told him as I walked over and carefully lifted her, passing my mate to her father. "I'll shift and follow."

"It will spook the horse. This is the fastest way to get her there. Do you remember where the waterfall is?"

"Yeah."

"Meet us there. If you prefer to shift, you will need to give us a head start."

I looked around the room as my warriors attempted to figure out the saddles. None of them had experience with preparing a horse.

"Go, we will follow shortly, keeping our distance."

He nodded and took off through the open barn door, flying into the night. I hated that I had to rely on Caspian to take her. I should be the one taking her. My wolf howled inside me from the pain, but I pushed it down and looked at my warriors.

I looked at my men, "Leave it. We will follow as our wolves. Whatever we do, we cannot spook the horse."

My legs had returned to me as we walked back out to the others. I needed to keep busy to stop myself from shifting right then and chasing after Caspian. The four previously injured Silver Ridge members were up on their feet and were being comforted by June. When I walked up, the woman holding the child rushed to me.

"Thank you, Alpha Forest. Your Luna has saved me and Olivia. We are eternally grateful to you both."

I forced a smile at her, too distracted about Juniper's well-being to give her my attention. Oliver and Jasper were

standing near Cain, giving him a hard time about fighting off
the rogues.

"Just couldn't wait until you got your wolf to find yourself
a rogue, huh, Cain?"

"Come on, what would you guys have done? The same
thing! You should have seen me, though. I would have had
them if they hadn't got a hold of my shoulder."

"Sure, little brother."

"Alpha Forest, will Juniper be alright?" Cain asked me in
a serious tone when he noticed me.

"Yeah..."

Their faces all dulled at my reaction.

"Should we go to her? Does she need us?" June offered.

"We will follow them in a minute. We're trying to let
Caspian get ahead of us before we shift."

She held her fists to her chest with worry. The conversation turned quiet as they all realized the severity of Juniper's
situation.

"We will go with you," Jasper stated sternly.

I nodded my head at him but turned away. My fists were
clenched as I held back my wolf. My need to be with Juniper
was beginning to drive me wild, and holding a conversation
would not happen. The whispering suddenly came to a halt.
I looked over at the others. Their faces were a mix of anger
and fear.

Alpha, the rogues are back, Oakley linked me. *They've
broken through the patrol.*

A roar escaped me as my shift took over. Juniper was out
there with only her father. They were in danger if the rogue
army had gotten past the patrol. I had to get to her. I had to
protect her.

12

Forest

W ith the threat to my mate, adrenaline-fueled my body as I raced toward the waterfall. I would not allow anyone to hurt her. I hadn't waited to find out from one of the Silver Ridge wolves what Caspian was doing. Would he turn back? Would he push forward? All I knew was that I had to find them. I could hear the others following behind me, but I was faster than them, and I pulled away.

I've directed the warriors to the fight, Oakley informed me. *We're unsure if any made it further onto pack ground.*

I have to get to Juniper. Her father took her to the waterfall.

We have this Alpha. Protect the Luna.

I trusted Oakley to handle the situation. There were nearly double the amount of warriors as there were rogues. It should be an easy battle, but I knew never to underestimate rogues. They fought dirty and would use any means necessary to win.

I ran through the meadow where we had left the cattle to graze. They took off when they spotted my wolf stampeding in the opposite direction. I paid them no mind as I turned up the winding trail. I hadn't found Caspian yet, but I could scent his horse, calming my worry that he had not been ambushed. The sound of falling water reached my ears as I neared the falls. The horse neighed and reared back. It was tied to a tree nearby. I shifted and ran past it, finding Caspian holding her in the pool of water. He looked up at me.

"Come take her; I have to help my pack," he hurriedly told me.

I dove into the water, reaching them quickly, and pulled her into my arms. The first feeling of relief hit my tense body from Juniper's contact. Thank the goddess she was safe.

They're retreating, Oakley called out.

Caspian must have heard the news as well. He turned back to me after he had left the pool.

"We need to check our territory to be sure none made it past them."

"The warriors I had with me are on the way. We will stay here to protect Juniper. My Beta will lead the rest of our men where you need them."

He nodded and took off, running past his horse. I knew he would be shifting, but I did not want to startle the animal further than I already had. I carried Juniper as deep as my feet reached, allowing the flowing water to glide its watery embrace around her. I was unsure how long it would take for her energy to return. It had taken nearly everything in her to heal the others. I heard footsteps approaching and found my warriors walking up to the pool.

"Stand guard," I told them. They spread out, keeping watch over their Alpha and Luna.

There, we stayed for what felt like hours. Oakley had informed me that they had found one rogue wandering towards the pack house. They captured him for interrogation and took him back to the pack house. We heard the all-clear come through the link. My shoulders relaxed, knowing that the rogues were gone. I still would not send my warriors away from the waterfall. I wouldn't risk Juniper being so vulnerable if they launched another attack.

With the first signs of dawn emerging in the sky, I felt Juniper begin to stir. My heart swelled as her eyes fluttered open. She looked groggy, but she continued to wake up.

"Forest," she breathed out.

I embraced her, "I'm here, Juniper."

She rested her head on my chest, allowing me to support her. After a few minutes, she lifted her head and looked around.

"You took my idea," she smiled up at me.

"What do you mean?"

"I figured I could use the waterfall to recharge."

"I have to give the credit to your father. I had only suggested a stream."

"You knew, though. You always know what I need."

She laid her head back down on my chest as she rested.

Juniper

FOREST WARMED my body with his own as we stood in the cool water, but I could tell we must have been there for some time. Even though I could feel his warmth, his skin felt like ice. I tried to pull back, wanting him to climb out so that he could warm up. He could shift so that his fur would blanket him. However, he kept his arms tight around me.

"Forest," I said as I looked up at him. "You need to let me go. I'm going to swim into the falls. The energy is strongest there."

"Then I'll go with you," he stated.

"You need to shift and warm up."

"Not if you don't," he said sternly.

He could be so stubborn sometimes. I lifted my dress over my head and attempted to toss it to the shore, followed by my bra and underwear. He watched me carefully as I dove in, swimming underwater up the turbulent current. I could feel the water pushing me down as I swam underneath the falls, the electrical charge slicing into me as it had done before. I surfaced on the back side of it, pulling myself up onto the small rock step that lay hidden underneath. Forest's head popped up beside me. He looked around as I pulled him up on the step.

"Is this where you disappeared to before?"

I smiled at him as I leaned my head back into the water. I could feel my body come alive with the sensation. Forest's arm wrapped around my waist, steadying me. I stayed there, allowing the cascade of churning water to revitalize me. When I stood back up, Forest pulled my body tight to his, slamming his mouth on mine. I succumbed to his need, my body giving itself entirely to him as we wrapped our arms tightly around each other, feeling like we needed to be even closer than two bodies pushed into each other. We needed to become one. His soft, plump lips were like pillows beckoning me to them, never to leave. When he finally pulled away, I took a sharp breath in.

"I was so worried about you," he said softly.

I ran my hand down his wet face, "I told you to have faith."

"There was an attack. The rogues broke through; Your father had ridden off with you alone. I had no idea if they had ambushed him. I can't lose you, Juniper."

My stomach clenched at his confession.

"I'm so sorry, Forest. That must have been terrifying."

He leaned his forehead against mine. I could feel his fear through the bond, and I countered it with my love for him, wanting him to feel every ounce of how much he meant to me.

"We're safe, Forest. Both of us."

He let out a breath of relief. I held him in my arms, allowing him to feel everything he needed to. As an Alpha, he could never show weakness. He had been scared. Though others would have known the fear he would have felt, he could not be vulnerable. At that moment, just the two of us were hidden from the world in our own sanctuary, and I allowed him that vulnerability.

WE STEPPED out of the pool, and I grabbed my dress from the shore and wrung it out. I collected the rest of my stuff and tied it as I had done many times before. Forest led us down the trail, and I saw my dad's horse.

"Should we bring it back with us?" I asked him.

"Your clothes are soaked, and there's no saddle. I'm sure he will send someone back for it later."

"I don't want to risk it. Help me up," I told him as I grabbed its mane.

"I'd prefer to go back with you," he said as more of a statement than a request.

"You can ride too," I winked at him.

"No," he glared at me.

Realizing that I wouldn't give in, he stepped up to help. He hoisted me onto its back, and I adjusted slightly, finding my center.

"I'll see you back there."

"Could you at least put on your dress?"

"It's soaking wet. Besides, when will I ever get the chance again to ride a horse naked?" I laughed as I tapped my heels into the horse's side, beginning down the path.

I was not an accomplished rider, but I felt more in control riding the horse bareback than with the saddle. I could feel its aura and could make a connection with the mare. After I broke into the meadow, I gave it another good tap, and we took off. The sunrise was behind me as we galloped back to the pack with the wind whipping at my hair. I couldn't help but laugh at the freedom. I felt like Lady Godiva herself.

The towering rocky mountains and dense forest full of hidden secrets surrounded me as I rode past the first house. I was so bewitched by my ride that I did not care if anyone saw me in all my nude glory. It was empowering to ride with such confidence, even though I had no idea where it came from. Everything felt right at that moment. The only thing that could improve it was if Forest was here with me, but I could feel him coming up behind. Just like our game of cat and mouse, I ran from his wolf, waiting for him to pounce on me and ravage my body.

When I approached the barn, I pulled slightly on the

horse's mane to slow down. I caught sight of my family's familiar faces running over from the pack house.

"Oh, my goddess, child," June called out. "Caspian, give her your jacket."

The others turned around to give me privacy, but I still had no care. June rushed over with the thick wool and flannel jacket and passed it to me before putting her hand on the horse's neck to stop it. I slipped on the warm cloth and leaned down on the horse, sliding my legs over the side until I dropped to the ground. I gently whispered a thank you in its perched ear as I brushed its neck.

"What on earth were you thinking riding in like that?" June asked.

"I didn't want to leave the horse out there on its own," I smiled at her, still on my high from the ride.

My dad turned around, a look of pride on his face as he came over and took hold of the horse. A man ran out of the barn to lead it back to its home.

"I didn't know you were that good at riding," Cain taunted.

I laughed, "I didn't know either."

"Where is your mate?" June asked.

"He's coming," I nodded in the direction I had come.

She came and wrapped her arm over my shoulder and began to lead me, "Well, let's get you inside and find you some clothes."

I dug my heels in, "I want to wait for Forest."

June pursed her lips. I didn't know why she was so worked up over my state of undress. All shifters were nude in front of others at some point. I heard the thunder of paws coming up behind me and caught sight of Forest's massive black wolf leading a group towards us. I had known some of the warriors were around as I had picked up their scent when we were back at the pond, but I hadn't realized there were so many.

"There are some clothes in the chest by the barn," Caspian told them as they shifted back.

Forest pulled on a pair of grey sweats that left nothing to the imagination before joining us. The other warriors grabbed some pants and went for the pack house. I was caught by surprise when my dad stepped up and hugged me. Our relationship was still new, but I could feel his fatherly love for me. I hugged him back, enjoying his affection.

When he pulled back, he looked at me and said, "I was worried about you. Thank you for saving Cain and the others."

June wrapped her arms around both of us, "You saved them. Thank you, Juniper."

Warmth spread inside of me from their sincerity and gratitude. I could feel their love for me, and this truly felt like my family. While I had grown up with my Gran and my cousins, this felt like something more. Something I wanted to have with my own children. The same ping to my heart struck with the thought of children, as it did every time the subject came up. I quickly shook the thought from my mind, not wanting it to spoil what I had now.

I pulled back, and Forest wrapped his arm around my waist. Cain came up to us. I smiled at him as I saw the life that had returned to his face. He had been so close to death last night, and now you couldn't even tell that something had happened to him.

"You're looking better," I told him.

"All thanks to you, I'm told."

I shrugged my shoulders and grinned.

"You really are a blessing from the Moon Goddess," June admired.

I scratched the back of my head, "I wouldn't say that."

"Don't lessen who you are, Juniper," she said thoughtfully.

I knew Selene had told me I was special, but I didn't feel like it. I just felt like me. I was just the same girl who grew up in our small coven hidden deep in the mountains of Washington. I was no better than anyone else.

13

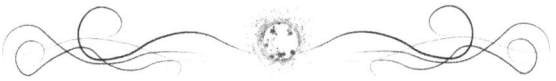

Forest

Juniper fought me when I asked her to rest today. She said that she felt fine and wanted to help the Silver Ridge Pack with cleaning. I had to block the doorway to stop her from pushing past me, resorting to pleading for her to relent finally. She needed rest, even if she didn't feel like it. Her body had been drained of all of its energy stores. While the water had helped, I was concerned for her. She finally conceded when she could sense my worry, but she made me promise that it would only be for the morning. She would keep her word with any luck, but I suspected she would slip out early.

Knowing I had done all I could to encourage Juniper to rest, I walked to Caspian's office. I knocked and waited for him to pull the door open. Oakley, Beta Leo, and Caspian's eldest, Jasper, were already inside. I joined them on the sofas so that we could discuss our plan.

"Is the Luna giving you a little trouble again?" Oakley teased me.

"You know her. She wants to be out helping the pack," I quipped back at him.

"June has it covered," Caspian added.

I shrugged, "I tried to tell her, but she is persistent. She finally agreed to rest for the morning, but we will see how long that will last."

"She is a Luna through and through," Caspian chuckled.

I shook my head as I surrendered to the truth. Even without being raised with our customs, Juniper perfectly fits the role of a Luna. She cared deeply about her pack and those she held dear. I knew she felt connected to the Silver Ridge Pack. It was, after all, her family's pack and where she would have been raised had she been born like the rest of us.

"Let's get this started," Caspian redirected. "Leo?"

Beta Leo stood up and walked over to a map on the wall of their territory.

"The rogues ~~have~~ attacked from both the south and east," he said, pointing to two spots marked on the map. "Their trail from the east will be the most recent, so we should start there and see where it leads. It will either lead us directly to their base camp or get a general idea of which direction to search."

"Didn't I hear that you were able to capture one?" I asked, leaning forward, my elbows resting on my knees.

"Yes, he's being held in the basement. We have secured cells down there," Caspian answered.

Most packs had some form of prison or holding cells. It was a place to hold unruly pack members or captured enemies.

"Have you tried talking to him?" I queried.

He frowned and shook his head, "He's refused to give anything up so far."

I rubbed my hand down my chin while I thought for a moment. "What tactics have you taken?" I asked.

Caspian held his hands behind his head as he leaned back, explaining, "He is being held in silver chains. We have withheld food and water for the time being."

I hummed before looking back at him, "Sometimes rogues will only respond with more *aggressive* methods."

"With all due respect, Alpha," Caspian sternly added, "we have handled our fair share of rogues before. More often than not, we have found that an aggressive approach right off the bat led the rogues to shut down. They're spiteful beings that would rather face death. A long and drawn-out tactic has received the best results. It is a slow torture that breaks them down."

"That may be, but perhaps our tactics are different. However, this is your pack and I will follow whatever choice you decide on," I relented.

"Thank you. I believe we should give it some time. Hopefully, it will all be a moot point after today," he replied.

CASPIAN and I stood at the front of the dining hall. The mess that we found yesterday had almost completely been cleaned up. The only evidence of the destruction left by the rogues were the boarded-up windows and the lingering sharp smell from the fire. It was a mix of a campfire and an acidic smell that stung my nostrils.

The warriors that had been selected to go after the rogues had gathered in front of us, listening intently to the plans that Caspian was detailing, "The rogues have only attacked at night so far, thus making us believe that they are sleeping during the day. We will take advantage of this and depart at 1300. We will follow their trail from last night in search of their camp. We will have scouts in front so we do not alert them of our approach. Once the camp is found, we will circle, attacking from all sides. Alpha Forest and I will be leading the attack. Wait for our signal."

He handed the floor over to me. I stepped forward and across the faces in front of me. The warriors were strong and well-trained. We should outnumber our enemy, hopefully minimizing casualties. One of the most vital skills we held over the rogues was the ability to work as a team, but there were two packs in front of me.

"Today, we will work as one. West Moon and Silver Ridge will fight as brothers rather than allies. Only together can we rid ourselves of this rogue army. If you see someone struggling, help them. Do not favor one side over the other. In addition, you will have two Alphas. You need to listen to both. Understood?" I announced.

"Yes, Alpha," the men before me chorused in unison.

"Go and prepare. We will meet in front of the pack house in two hours," Caspian called before closing the meeting.

"That was a good speech, Alpha Forest," Caspian said as we watched the room clear.

I grumbled, "They must remember to work as a team. Two packs, side by side. Otherwise, they may hinder one another rather than help."

"I couldn't agree more," Caspian nodded.

As we walked out, the kitchen crew began filtering in to begin lunch preparations. I caught sight of Juniper standing near the stairs, talking to some pack members. Caspian patted me on my back before turning down the hall towards his office. I walked up to her, listening in on her conversation.

"We won't leave until all of this is settled. You can rest assured," she told the woman next to her. "Until then, I'm sure Luna June can help your family find a place in the pack house if you feel safer."

My chest swelled with pride. She was truly the perfect Luna. She continued to comfort the woman as I wrapped my arm around her waist. The other woman lowered her head when she noticed me.

"Alpha Forest," she bowed.

"Hello," I replied.

"I will get it all sorted. Come and find me if there are any problems," Juniper told her.

"Thank you, Luna Juniper," the woman bowed again.

Juniper smiled at her before turning away to walk up the stairs with me. I was going to give her a hard time for being out of the room, but I couldn't bring myself to do it now, not after watching her console the woman.

"We have just over an hour until I need to be back to help prepare," I informed her.

She nodded, "You should make sure you eat before you go."

The corner of my lips curled upwards, "They're preparing lunch now."

"Good. We should ensure all the warriors have enough to eat before they go. Who knows how long you will be out there. You will all need to have the strength to fight the rogues."

We walked into our room, and I closed the door behind us.

"I will make sure of it," I assured her.

She turned around and placed her hands on my chest, peering up at me.

"I'm worried, Forest," she whispered.

I wrapped my hands around her hips, trying to convey my sincerity, "There is nothing to worry about."

"You're going off to fight a small army. There is plenty to worry about," she said firmly.

14

Forest

The men gathered in front of the pack house, conversing amongst themselves. Mates whispered their farewells as children ran around their father's legs. I stood to the side with my arms crossed over my chest and Juniper's arm wrapped around my waist. We watched the group grow in size as more and more pack members showed up. There was not an ounce of fear within them, only the sheer determination to eliminate the rogue threat.

Caspian came and stood at my side, "They look to be about ready."

"Agreed."

"We leave in five," he called out to the warriors.

"Where is June?" Juniper asked him.

"She will be here in a minute," he replied gently with a small smile.

I could tell he appreciated her asking about June.

He looked between us, "I will give you two a minute."

Juniper unwrapped her arm from me and hugged her father.

"You be safe out there," she said softly.

"I always try," he smiled before returning to the house.

I was sure he was going to find June before we left.

I pulled Juniper to me, "Stay in the pack house while we are gone."

"I will," she said before kissing me.

I leaned my forehead against hers and pushed a stray curl out of her face, tucking it behind her ear.

I love you, I linked her, just between the two of us.

I love you, too. Promise me you will be safe.

I promise.

She kissed me deeply once more before taking a step back. I turned towards the men and called them over. Caspian joined me once more as I watched June come up beside Juniper and wrap her arm around her shoulders. I was grateful for the comfort that she gave her in my absence.

Caspian stepped forward to address the entire pack, "We suggest that all families make their way to the pack house while we are away. Twenty warriors will be stationed around the perimeter, and another ten will be on patrol watching our borders. As for those who will be joining Alpha Forest and myself. We head east. Now let's go!"

With that, Caspian shifted, shredding his clothing. I followed suit and left one of my last pairs of pants in rags scattered across the trampled lawn. Together, we took off, leading the charge. The sound of bones cracking and cloth tearing informed us that our warriors followed our lead as we raced together as one to find the rogues.

We reached the border quickly, picked up their scent, and began following the trail, which led deeper into the sloping mountains.

Alpha, one of my scouts linked me—*the trail heads in two directions.*

We're on our way.

We reached a wild river that tore a path through the stone-encrusted landscape. As we scented around, we found that their trails split. Some went north, while others traveled south. I shifted back and knelt to inspect their tracks. Caspian followed suit as we took in their separation. Our warriors created a wall of protection behind us due to our vulnerability.

"Do you think there are two camps?" he asked.

I shook my head, "No. I think they are trying to throw us off."

"We shouldn't risk splitting the group."

"It may be the only way for us to find where they went," I argued.

"We can head north first, together. If they are not there, we try again tomorrow and head south," Caspian insisted.

I rubbed the side of my chin as I stood and assessed the area.

"The trail would weaken by then. We need to split. I will lead a group to the south; you take the north. We split our men evenly so that we could still communicate. Once we find where they are, we report to the other group and wait until we merge again before we attack."

Caspian's brows furrowed, "They could be waking by then."

"They could be, but it would be better to take them on their own turf than risk them attacking your pack again."

He watched me for a moment before nodded in agreement and shifted back. I surveyed the area once more before shifting back into my own wolf.

The trail splits. I need two equal groups. Beta Oakley will travel with Alpha Caspian and one group heading north, while I will lead the group heading south. We will report when we find them. We do not attack until we meet back up, I linked my men.

Yes, Alpha, they replied.

I watched as they split into two groups, just like the Silver Ridge Warriors. They were swift, and within minutes, we were on our way. We skirted through the pine forest, leaping our way through the rock outcroppings and navigating up and down the rock faces that littered the area. The stench of rogue diluted the rich scent of the forest.

As we approached a large rock face, the trail again split. They were bright for rogues. After our initial split, we were already in groups of just over thirty warriors. It was still large enough that we could potentially take the rogues on if needed, but to dwindle us down to a mere fifteen would put each group at risk.

Oakley, I linked, *our trail split again.*

I will inform Alpha Caspian.

I waited while he communicated my information. Beta Leo, who had traveled with me, and I shifted so we could talk.

"We should split and go after them," he said.

"Let's see what Caspian thinks. Oakley is talking with him now."

He said we could regroup and send scouts ahead, Oakley linked me back.

If they are found, they stand no chance against us united. We are better off splitting the group and reforming quickly rather than giving them more time to prepare.

Another delay came as he relayed my response.

He says it's your call.

I was hesitant, but it was the best plan to find their camp. We had already traveled many miles, and if we turned back now, we would have missed the opportunity to surprise them. Splitting would allow us to scout the areas and call the others safely. I would be surprised if it were much further.

I contacted Oakley, *Beta Leo will lead one group, and I will take the other. We will designate a leader from each pack to accompany the other.*

Yes, Alpha.

"We will be splitting. Select one man to be your point man in my group. You will lead the other," I informed Beta Leo.

He gave me a quick nod, "Yes, Alpha Forest."

I looked back at the warriors and said, "We will be splitting again. This is now a scouting mission. Travel in stealth and be sure that you are not seen. Silas will be my point man in Beta Leo's group."

"Parker will be mine," Beta Leo added.

"Split into two even groups. We need to move quickly."

With my smaller group, we continued on the rogue's trail. With the split of their numbers, the strength of the trail waned. We had to move slower to stay on it. With time passing, we began to risk the chance that the rogues would wake soon, making the situation even more dire if they spotted us.

A break in the shadows gave way to a meadow. I signaled the others to lay low as I inspected it for signs of the enemy. I crawled on my belly as I approached. The bright golden grasses swayed with the breeze as I watched for movement. I did not see a camp, but that did not mean they weren't hidden beneath the grass cover. Even if they were not in there, crossing the meadow would expose us to any rogue scouts. Their scent went directly into the field, making me even more cautious. I crawled back to the others and shifted, staying low within the cover of the trees.

"The trail leads into the meadow. We will travel the exterior, splitting into two teams. Parker will lead the one to the right, and I will lead the one to the left. If you catch their scent leaving the meadow, report it to the other group. Stay low and stay on guard," I told the group.

While I despised splitting my numbers even further, we would still be within range to help one another.

Before we could split and make way, Oakley linked me, *Our trail has split as well. They went in three directions. We will break into three groups and scout them out.*

Have Reed and West take point in the other two groups.

Yes, Alpha.

As if on cue, Silas linked me immediately after I ended my conversation with Oakley.

Alpha, the trail split again. What would you like us to do?

My frustration grew. How far were we willing to scatter ourselves?

Put Heron as Point with Beta Leo. If it splits again, then we call it and regroup, I tell him, my frustration growing.

Yes, Alpha.

I looked back at the men in front of me who were waiting for my orders.

"Let's go."

I shifted back and led my team around the meadow, sticking to the cover of the forest so as not to give our location away. I picked up the putrid scent of rogue leaving the meadow and heading back into the forest, but it was less potent than the one that had entered, leading me to believe they had split again.

I linked my warriors with Parker and informed them, telling them to continue as planned to see if we could find any more trails. We continued, wrapping around the golden void of the meadow, picking up another rogue trail along the way. We found four trails leading out when we converged at the far end—four individual trails. There was no way for us to track them. They had outsmarted us. I growled in frustration.

Alpha, our trail split again, Heron reported.

I broadcast to all of my warriors on the mission, *The trails continue splitting. We cannot track them unless we follow each individual trail. We need to regroup and come up with a new plan. We will meet back at the river where we first split.*

I led my group back around the meadow the way we had come. It had become a wild goose chase and one we could not win. We would have to find a way to get a step ahead of them.

Caspian says he still has a strong trail and wants to continue following it, Reed reported.

We will reconvene with our group and head north to support him.

Yes, Alpha.

If he still had a good trail, perhaps it could lead us somewhere. It was a better chance than anything we had on our end. Hours had been wasted following each trail, and we needed to make something happen. We climbed up the hill away from the valley.

Forest! Juniper screamed in my head, *we are being attacked!*

Everyone back to the pack! The rogues are attacking, I bellowed through the link as I broke into a frantic sprint to return to my mate.

15

Juniper

J une and I had been busy setting up the pack house for the families. Most had already made their way here, but a few had returned to their homes to collect some of their things in case they needed to stay the night. I used this time to help the shattered mates. It was not nearly the drain that healing the critically wounded took from me. June busied herself preparing dinner for the pack while others moved mattresses around. They had a store of inflatable beds to use in such situations. When I finished my tasks, I walked out to the front of the pack house and looked off in the distance, wishing I would see Forest's wolf emerge from the trees.

"Luna," one of the warriors who had stayed to protect us said as he lowered his head.

"Hi Dustin, any news?" I asked, hopeful.

"Not yet," he replies, noting my disappointment.

I continued watching as the minutes passed by. I had nearly given up when I caught movement in the trees. Wolves, lots of them. They were racing back to us. My heart fluttered with relief that Forest was returning. I began walking forward, wanting to run to him upon his return, but my feet stopped. I couldn't feel him. He was not with the group of wolves who came through the forest. None of my pack was.

Just as they broke through the trees, I yelled out to my mate, *Forest! We are being attacked!*

The warriors caught sight of them and shifted as they rushed forward, taking them head-on. The field in front of the pack house quickly turned into a battlefield full of bloodshed as wolf tore into wolf. Growls and barks chorused through the air. Screams from inside the house reminded me of what I had to do. I rushed inside, finding June already bolting the rear doors.

"Is everybody inside?" I asked her with panic in my voice.

"I don't think so... Fleur and her daughter went back for her stuffed animal," she gasped with realization.

Her eyes glazed over as she linked to Fleur, I assumed.

I waited as her face turned from panic to horror.

"They were walking back. I told her to hide in her house."

"I will go after them. Lock the pack house. When I get back, I will knock five times," I said as I started back toward the front door.

I couldn't risk them being found and injured or, worse, killed.

"No, you can't! It's too dangerous. There are too many of them," she yells, grabbing my arm.

I stopped and stared deeply into her eyes. "I am going,

June. Do not try to stop me. It will only put me at a greater risk. The wolves are distracted by the warriors. I can slip out before they notice me."

She threw her hand over her mouth and nodded. Tears glistened in her eyes, but she was letting me go, even through her internal protest.

"Where is their house?" I asked before I walked away.

"She lives in the green house with the blue door, south of here. It's towards the entrance."

"Lock up the house. I will be back as soon as I can."

I ran to the front door and peeked out. The battle outside still raged on. The warriors were holding their own against the rogues. I slipped out and stuck close to the shrubs in front of the pack house. I watched for a moment, taking note of the reasonably even numbers. There were supposedly forty rogues, but I only saw around twenty-five. Where could the rest of them be?

I didn't have time to answer my question, so I raced away from the pack house, shifting when I was clear of sight. As I took in the houses scattered before me, I noticed blackness drifting up to the cloudless sky. I ran even harder, realizing that I was seeing smoke coming from the family houses, right where Fleur and her daughter were hiding. I could hear the shattering of glass coming from the buildings ahead of me, so I took shelter behind a home nearby. The rogues weren't just attacking the pack house this time; they were going after the surrounding homes. I had to stop them, but first, I needed to ensure that Fleur and her daughter were safe.

Forest, they have around twenty-five attacking the pack house and more burning down the family homes, I linked quickly.

Stay in the pack house. We are coming as fast as we can, he replied, his voice filled with anger and worry.

I'm at the houses. One of the mothers and her daughter came to get something left behind, I tell him.

Dammit...Then, stay hidden, he says.

If only I could promise him I would. I looked across the houses tucked along the road and spotted Fleur's up ahead. The rogues were in their human forms with satchels strewn over their shoulders. I watched as they pulled a bottle out and uncorked it. They shoved a soiled rag inside before lighting it up with the flick of a lighter. I watched a man toss it through a window, igniting the home inside. His laughter echoed off of the buildings. How could anyone be so cruel and heartless?

Another man walked towards Fleur's home. My breath caught as I realized they were about to do the same thing to hers. I couldn't let it happen. I jumped out of my hiding spot and growled at them. They turned to face me, their faces morphing into a mix of evil satisfaction and psychotic glee.

"Look what we have here, boys," The man in front of Fleur's house said.

More men walked out from behind the other houses nearby. I counted ten in all who gathered in front of me.

"A little she-wolf who thinks she has some cajones," he went on.

"Maybe she's just looking for a little ride of her own," another one chimed in.

"Perhaps, but I think we have a high rank here. She's probably here to rescue her pack," the first man chuckled darkly.

They all laughed as they mocked me, but I wouldn't let their words affect my focus. I may not be a fighter, but I would do whatever I could to protect the innocent mother and child from their wrath. I growled again, but that only brought on another wave of laughter.

The man who initially talked to me handed his bag to the one beside him, "Here, take this. Let me see how wild she can be."

He looked back at me and licked his lips before he shifted into a mangy-looking grey and tan wolf. He growled at me before lunging. I dove to my right and whipped my head back, nipping at his leg. I could taste the slight coppery tang of blood, but my grip had not been firm enough for me to hold him. He growled again and jumped at me, biting onto my foot as I attempted to evade him once more. I yelped with pain and shook my foot, but he had a firm hold. I twisted my head back and latched onto his shoulder, shaking my head violently. I could feel his skin tear within my jaws. This would sicken me any other time, but I had no time to think about it. It was a fight for survival.

Juniper, what's happening? Forest called through the link.

I could not respond. It took every ounce of concentration to fight the shifter before me. With my firm hold on his shoulder, he released my paw and jerked backward, breaking away from me but leaving a mouth full of flesh behind. I stepped down on my back foot and winced in pain. Keeping it raised, I squared up again. I knew I would never be able to defeat all the rogues facing me, so I called forth a shield. If I could at least keep them at bay until others could come to help, then I just might stand a chance.

Sruth cumhachd, cruthaich balla. Dìon mi bhon nàmhaid gun chrìoch, I chanted in my mind as I lowered my head, directing it in front of me.

It was a risky move. Usually, we would use our hands to

guide the energy, but with only paws, I had to use the only other option available: my head. Lowering it seemed like a sign of weakness and opened me to attack if the spell failed or if he broke through it. I could hear the rogues laughing, but I growled in return, lifting my gaze back up to them. It would work better if I could continue the directional push, but it was established, and I needed to face them so they knew I was not submitting.

As it caught my determined eyes, the wolf charged again, slamming into the unseen barrier. He yelped, and blood began trickling down his snout.

"What the hell?" One of them shouted. "Go again, Tyler."

The wolf reared back before charging as hard as he could. His head collided with the shield again, but this time, at the exact moment of impact, I forced my power into the shield and drove it forward sharply. The impact was like running into a speeding truck, and a cracking sound rang out, caused by his neck snapping. He dropped to the ground, lifeless. I could tell the spell had weakened and would not take another blow. With the death of their comrade, the other wolves dropped their bags and shifted. They were more enraged now than ever, with a bloodlust to take my life. Only one was left standing in his human form.

"We were going to go easy on you. Maybe have a little fun and then let you go. After killing Tyler, we won't be so friendly. We will pass you around like a bottle of cheap whiskey. We will fuck you until your last breath and leave your body parts on your borders for your Alpha to find."

A dangerous shiver ran up my spine from his threat. The best bet that I would have would be to shift back to my human form and throw a fireball at them as I had with the

Wendigo last winter. My bones rearranged as I shifted back, exposing myself to the rogues.

The one who was still in man form licked his lips, "That's better. It will go a lot easier if you don't fight."

I held my chin up high and stared at him directly in the eyes as a challenge, "I will never submit to a piece of scum like you."

His smile turned into a scowl as he took in my threat. He shifted into a mangy beast of his own and growled at me.

I readied myself when a whisper flew to me on the breeze, *"Bring your fire to your wall..."*

I had heard her enough times to know when Selene was guiding me. I let her wisdom enter my body and focused as the words flowed through me like water trickling down a brook. I closed my eyes and chanted in whispers as a wall of fire encircled me. I could feel its warmth. It was not a danger to me but a comfort.

The wolves jumped back and watched me with bewilderment. It was only a fleeting moment of hesitation on their part before they began launching themselves at me. With my spell cast, I shifted back as the first one slammed into my protective shield, its fur bursting into flames. It ran off, screaming out its wolfish howl. The others circled me, still prepared to attack. Another jumped forward, attempting to get over the fire's height, but as its back paw touched the flames, he, too, ignited, falling into the protected space within. I evaded him as he raced around, looking for a way out. After what felt like an eternity, but in reality, it was only seconds, he collapsed to the ground, a charred husk.

As the others began to step back, a ferocious howl ripped through the clearing, and I knew that Forest had arrived. Forest charged ahead, taking on the shifter who had taunted me. The wolf turned and tried to grab hold of Forest's throat for the immediate kill, but Forest halted as he lunged, and the other shifter's teeth slammed shut before their mark. It allowed Forest to grab him by the shoulder, crunching down and snapping the bones like twigs. Blood spurted out from the sides of his mouth, spilling across the gravel road.

A group of warriors charged in just as the other six wolves set their sights on Forest. Oakley took on another wolf, biting its legs as it leaped for Forest's back. The warriors outnumbered the rogues by thirteen. It made easy work for them to slay with little effort. The wolf that had fought Forest lay unconscious at his feet. I could still see his chest moving slightly with labored breaths. With the situation resolved, I dropped the protective barrier and limped to Forest. He sniffed at my foot and licked at it.

We need to get Fleur and her daughter out of the green house, I told him.

I could tell he linked Oakley as I saw him take off to the house, shifting as he came to the door and called out her name. I watched with worry until the curtains pulled back an inch, and Fleur's face peeked out. When she saw Oakley, she opened the door and thanked him for coming for them. Her three-year-old daughter, Daisy, followed her out.

"Do you have some spare clothes for the Alpha and Luna?" I heard him ask her.

"Yes, give me a minute," she said before returning inside.

A moment later, she brought out a pile of clothing and handed it to Oakley. He ran it over towards us as Forest shifted. He took the clothing and pulled on a pair of sweats that were too short for him. Everyone turned away from us.

"You can shift now."

I didn't know his reasoning, but I did as he said. My

crimson fur disappeared within my skin as my bones popped and broke back into place. I stood on one foot, steadying myself on him as he helped slide a loose-fitted floral sundress over my head. Once I was dressed, he picked me up in his arms.

"Let's get back to the pack house," he called out.

16

Juniper

Six pack wolves had been lost in the surprise battle with the rogues. Half were from the Silver Ridge Pack, while the remaining three were from mine. They had slaughtered the four wolves on patrol, killing them before they could send the warning. They had hidden on the banks of a river to conceal their scent and used arrows to silently kill them, decapitating the bodies afterward to be sure they had fulfilled their vile mission. It all felt like something I would have read in some historical novel, bow and decapitation, rather than in our present-day world.

The use of weapons amongst shifters was highly frowned upon and deemed a cowardly way to fight. The animals within us thrived on hand-to-hand or claw-and-tooth combat. Weapons were considered the human way of fighting, and it was one of the shifter's founding rules that separated us from them.

The other two lost pack wolves died in the battle at the

pack house. We were fortunate that they had split their forces to burn the homes, though the destruction damaged the spirit of many of the Silver Ridge pack members. The local fire department was dispatched after someone driving nearby saw the smoke billowing from the pack land. They will be nearby over the next few days investigating but had already said it appeared to be arson. If only they knew the true brutality of it. We would need to keep everyone away from the area for the time being. June and some other women have worked tirelessly to prepare the pack house. Whole families to a room, filling each one until they could begin to rebuild.

The more significant pressing matter was the fact that many of the rogues had escaped. And here we were, yet again, gathered in my father's office, hashing out ideas and theories on our next steps.

"We have counted fourteen rogues in total that were killed, plus one taken captive by Alpha Forest," Beta Leo reported.

"It was a setup. They were waiting for us to be far enough away so they could attack without interruption," Caspian spat out in disgust. "They go after our women and children rather than face us like wolves."

"They will be held accountable," Forest stated firmly.

"Yes, but how? We still have no idea where their camp is. Do we just wait for them to come and pick off more of our own?"

My father was angry, as was I.

"We are lucky that Juniper was able to hold off the group that went after the houses," Oakley added. "It allowed us to take out ten more."

"And lucky enough that she could wield her power to

hold them back until Alpha Forest and the rest of you showed up. If not, I would have lost not only more pack members but also my own daughter," Caspian growled out.

At this point, everyone was venting their frustration. They were livid and determined to kill every last one of them.

"If we have something of theirs, I can try to find them," I offered.

"They have left nothing," Beta Leo added.

"Not even a scrap of fur?" I pushed, scraping for ideas.

Leo shook his head, "You would be hard-pressed to decipher which fur belonged to what person."

"I could try. It may take a few attempts, but perhaps I can find something," I said, hoping to give us an advantage.

"What about the banished warrior?" Forest added. "He must have left something."

"You're right," Caspian said. "Their house was not torched like the others."

Within an instant, all the men were up and rushing out the door to get to Callan's place. My ankle and foot were still sore, so I stayed seated on the sofa. I was sure that they would return soon enough. June came over and joined me.

"I wanted to thank you again for going after Fleur. I don't know what I would have done if we had lost her and her child," she said, her voice filled with gratitude.

I took her hand and said, "You never have to thank me for something like that. It is what anyone would have done."

"No, sweetheart. It's not. You showed bravery most of us only wished we had," she said, tightening her grip on my hand.

I gulped, "You would have gone."

She smiled weakly at me, "I would have if I could. Being

the Luna has repercussions, as you know. We have to make difficult decisions. I had to choose between Fleur and the rest of the women. If you had not been here, there would have been no hope for them."

Her admission to what she had chosen settled deep in my gut, like a boulder sitting in my stomach. I had not been in a position where I had to make a choice like that, and I feared the day I was.

We sat in silence until the men returned sometime later. Caspian clutched at a ratted and stained red shirt.

"Will this do?" he asked urgently.

I jumped up from my spot on the sofa, "Yes! I need a quartz crystal, a glass of water, and a map."

Jasper and Beta Leo hurried out of the room to collect the remaining items.

"Why had we not done this earlier?" Oakley asked.

I dropped my head, feeling like I could have avoided this whole fight, "I hadn't thought about it until now. I was taught how to do the spell when I was young, but I had little use for living in the coven with everyone I knew."

Sensing my disappointment, Forest replaced June beside me and grabbed my hand with his, nearly wrapping around the whole thing with its size.

"We can do it now," he said encouragingly.

I bit my lip and nodded my head. I looked around the room, hoping I did not find the same disappointed looks I felt within myself, yet no one seemed upset. I felt relieved that they were not judging me for my mistake.

Jasper and Beta Leo returned, placing everything I needed on the coffee table in front of me. I rolled the map out, ensuring it sat according to the cardinal directions. The north end of the map had to be on the north side, south at the south, and so on. I placed the glass of water on the edge of the northern side and held the shirt in my left hand.

"Do you have some string or something similar?"

"Here, you can use my boot lace," Jasper offered as he undid his laces.

I tied it to the end of the crystal and held the other end of the lace in my right hand, hovering over the center of the map. I briefly glanced at Forest, who smiled encouragingly at me.

I closed my eyes and began to chant, "*Selene, mo mhàthair, treòraich mi gu sealbhadair an nì seo gus am faighear e.*"

I opened my eyes back up and blew lightly on the crystal. It swung outwards and back before turning in a circular motion. It moved further to the southeast, so I guided my hand closer to that direction. When it began to center, I stilled my hand, watching as it turned slower and slower. I lowered my hand steadily until the tip touched a place on the map.

"They're on the far side of Deep End Lake," Caspian whispered.

"At least Callan is," Leo added.

"Then we will take him out first," Caspian said with determination.

"Have you had any luck with the prisoners?" Forest asked my dad.

"Not yet. I fear that you may be right. While I still think that waiting will give us the better outcome, now that we have two, we could try a different tactic with the new one."

"We do that first. Everyone needs to rest. If we find out anything, we can make adjustments from there, but I say we head out at first light tomorrow," Forest said.

Caspian agreed, as did everyone else. I was thankful to

call it a night and stood up, favoring my good foot. Forest scooped me up in his arms to carry me out.

"I can walk, you know," I chuckled at him.

He grunted, "I do. I also know that it hurts you to do so."

"It doesn't matter," I whispered.

"It does," he said sternly.

"I will get Juniper settled, and I will meet you in the basement to help with the interrogation," he said to Caspian.

My father gave him a nod and said, "We will wait for you before we begin."

I called goodnight to the rest of them before Forest whisked me away. I didn't argue with him further about carrying me. It was a relief not to endure the pain of walking up the stairs. When we entered our room, he gently placed me on the bed, went into the bathroom, and turned on the shower. When he returned, he helped me and pulled the sundress over my head.

"I think I can undress on my own," I teased him.

A mischievous smirk formed on the corner of his mouth, "Where's the fun in that?"

He slipped off his clothes and carried me into the shower. He helped support me as I leaned back in the water, savoring the glorious relief I felt from the cleansing. I dared not look down at the filth that washed off of me. I had seen enough of its evidence on my arms and hands. My fight with the rogues had tossed me wildly over the loose, dry dirt. I had attempted to wash up with our return earlier, but I knew only a shower would take it all away.

Forest poured shampoo into his hand before lathering it and working it through my tangled locks. He used the hand sprayer to rinse the suds from my head. As he began his work with the conditioner, I ran my hands down his sculpted chest.

He clicked his tongue at me, "None of that, my mate; you need to rest."

"What I need is you," I said huskily, determined, as I looked up at him with a sultry gleam in my eyes.

He wrapped his slick hands down my waist and pulled me flush to him, pressing his lips hard onto mine. His tongue pushed through my parted lips, sweeping across my mouth and tangling with my own tongue. A moan forced its way up my throat as a new warmth grew inside of me. I ran my hand down his stomach until I found my intended target, grasping ahold of it. I used the water and soap to slide my hand up and down, circling my thumb around the tip.

He pushed me backward until my back met the smooth, cool stone. Lifting my injured leg, I wrapped it around his thigh as he slid his hand down, pushing his finger into me. I gasped out at the welcome intrusion and moaned as I leaned my forehead against him as my body gave itself away. Right as I neared the cusp of relief, he pulled back. I looked at him concerned, worried that something had happened, but I only found a lustful, mischievous grin.

He turned me around, the water cascading down my back as he entered me from behind. My fingers splayed across the smoothed tile as I moaned out with pleasure. His hand reached around, playing as he built me back up. I came quickly, bending further into the spraying water. My toes curled in, and my fists clenched as the euphoria spread throughout my body like an electrical charge. Goosebumps littered my skin even after I began to recover.

"Forest, make me come again. Please," I begged him.

I could hear his moan of pleasure as he increased his

movements. My already sensitive core reveled in the bliss it received. I could feel he was close himself, but he brought me back to my high. My body trembled as it came unraveled. Each muscle gained a mind of its own as I pushed back into him, craving for him to be deeper. With nowhere else to hold, my hands wrapped around one another as if they were in a celebratory embrace. He filled me as he, too, tipped over the edge of pleasure and satisfaction.

He turned me around and kissed me deeply. I could feel every ounce of his love and admiration for me. I did not want our embrace to end, but with more important matters at hand, he pulled back.

"I love you, Juniper," he said wholeheartedly.

"I love you too, Forest," I replied.

He helped me clean up and finish rinsing the conditioner from my hair before turning the water off and wrapping me tightly in a plush white towel. I ran my fingers through my curls, fighting the tangles that had grown throughout the day. He lifted me back into his arms and carried me to the bed. Pulling my pajamas out of the dresser, he helped me dress before tucking me in. With one final kiss, I watched him leave, heading down to interrogate the prisoners.

17

Forest

I made my way down to the darkened basement, finding Caspian and Jasper already there. I was surprised to see his son. Interrogations were not for the weak-hearted, and he was still young.

"Are you sure you want him here for this?" I said to Caspian.

"It's time he learned," Caspian said firmly.

I would not stand in the way of an Alpha training his successor, even if my own opinions differed. Caspian led us into a small room where Oakley and Leo stood on either side of the recently captured rogue. He was seated in a steel chair with his hands tied behind his back. A thick corded rope kept his body restrained to the chair, and a pair of silver cuffs shackled him at his feet, preventing him from shifting. Caspian dragged another chair from the corner, placing it in front of him a few feet back.

"We have a few questions for you. I hope that you can comply."

The rogue spat at him, missing his mark.

"Let's see if we can change your mind."

He nodded at Leo, who stepped forward and punched forcefully into his stomach. The breath escaped him, and the chair flew backward, slamming into the concrete flooring.

He coughed hard, but as soon as he regained his breath, he spat out, "Go eat shit."

Leo and Caspian never relented in their physical interrogation for nearly an hour. The rogue was bloodied and bruised. His face was swollen, yet he had not given us a single bit of information. I cleared my throat, signaling them to step out. We all walked into the hallway, closing the door behind us.

"I told you it is difficult to gain any information using physical force," Caspian exasperated.

"How about I give it a go?" I said, popping my knuckles.

Caspian shook his head but said, "Be my guest, but I would be surprised if you can break him."

The corner of my lip tilted up. Challenge excepted. I was not a cruel man, but I would do what needed to be done to protect my pack and the packs that I was allied with. These rogues had killed some of my warriors and attacked my mate. All kindness had to be removed from the room in order to accomplish our goal.

We stepped back in and slammed the door behind us. The rogue lifted his head and smirked through his bloodied teeth.

"I'm ready for more when you are," he spat out.

The problem with Caspian's methods was that they were too nice. Our kind were used to getting beaten up. We trained in fighting constantly, even in the rogue groups. The uneven tempers often led to fights. Injuries did not scare us. We healed quickly and were used to pain.

I sat down in the chair across from him.

"Changing the lineup, I see," he goated.

I leaned back and crossed my arms, refraining from giving him the satisfaction of a reply.

The rogue chuckled, "Ah, the tough Alpha. You're the one who came to save his mate. It's such a pity. We had a real good plan on what to do with her."

A fire burned within me, but I held it at bay.

"Your mate has a nice set of tits, too," he ran his tongue across his lips. " I bet she's wild in the sack, huh?"

Caspian stepped forward, but I shot him with a look of warning. Right then, I knew that even if we needed more information, this man would not be leaving this room alive. I looked over at Oakley and nodded my head. He reached into his back pocket and brought a large pair of pruning shears.

I leaned forward, resting my elbows on my knees, "Perhaps I can help you with that mouth of yours. What should we start with first?"

I could see him grind his teeth together, unwilling to risk dismemberment. More than likely, he had already accepted his fate. He knew he was going to die, but he could choose how it would be. Quick or painfully slow.

"What are you getting for helping attack the pack?" I asked him.

His lips stayed sealed tight.

I looked at Oakley and nodded again. He stepped forward, grabbing ahold of his foot.

"We will start small, maybe a pinky toe? No...that's too

easy. And my Beta here is not great with the small ones. We'll take a couple at once. What do you say?"

His silence remained.

"Too easy, huh? I know one part that no man wants to go without. Without it, you're not really a man anymore..."

Oakley moved upwards, finding his manhood, and opened the pruners.

"Wait," he shouted. "We were going to take over the pack."

I leaned back again, "There's no Alpha in your group. We all know what happens to an Alpha-less pack."

"The plan was to take one of his sons. Keep him captive until we could train him ourselves. Callan would lead until then."

"Do you actually think that Callan would have stepped down after assuming the role?"

"We had a deal. A pack with an Alpha. If he didn't step down, someone, most likely the Alpha, would have challenged him," he continued to explain.

I scoffed, "He would have killed the Alpha to keep control."

"No," he said adamantly.

Knowing he was so desperate to return to a pack, he would have accepted any lie Callan laid out; I changed directions, "Why were you banished?"

I needed to keep him talking. Focusing on simple questions would get him comfortable before asking the more relevant ones -ones we needed to take down.

He growled and looked away, a telling sign that whatever it was - it was terrible.

"No need to answer. It doesn't matter. How many of you are there?"

He stared at me with contention. I nodded at Oakley, who returned to his task.

"Wait!" he called again with a growl. "There were forty-two of us last I checked."

"Where are you guys camped?"

"Southeast of here, near a lake."

Juniper's spell had worked; he had just confirmed it.

"What's their next step?" I asked further.

"The plan was to dwindle you down. It would have been easy if you all hadn't shown up," he said through his gritted teeth."

"How exactly were you going to do that?"

"We have scouts around your borders watching to see if you leave. That's how we knew you were gone today. We waited until you were far enough away before they called in the attack."

"We haven't caught the scent of anyone nearby."

"They're perched on the mountains nearby with binoculars. It's not that hard to see."

So they had been watching us.

"Which mountains?'

"I don't know their names. There's one to the north, two to the east and south."

"What about the West?"

"Too close to the town. We couldn't find one close enough to get a good sight."

"When will they attack again?" I pushed further.

"Depends..." he said hesitantly.

"On what?"

He locked his eyes on me, "What you do next."

I took a breath, loosening my muscles. I needed him to keep talking.

"Give it a shot. If you had to say, when would it be?" I asked easily.

He shook his head but said, " Probably sometime in the next three days."

"Any chance they will attack tonight?"

"Doubtful. With our loss in numbers, Callan will want to regroup."

I stood from my chair, "I appreciate your cooperation."

I walked behind him and grabbed his head with my arm, twisting it firmly until the sickening sound of his neck breaking told me he was dead.

"Did you have to kill him?" Jasper asked.

I cocked an eyebrow at him, "Did you hear what he said about your sister?"

He dropped his head. It was a death sentence to talk about a Luna that way. I had shown him mercy by making it quick—more than he deserved. As we returned to Caspian's office, two warriors cleaned up the room and disposed of the rogue's body. He would be buried somewhere off lands when the opportunity arose, along with the others. The lost pack members would have an honorary funeral to celebrate their lives.

"I noticed you didn't use force," Caspian said as we entered.

"There was no need," I grinned back at him.

I could see the corner of his mouth tilt up, "I believe our tactics in physical interrogation differ."

"Let it be known that I never want to be interrogated by the West Moon Pack," Leo said as he took his seat, his hand adjusting his manhood.

"Would you have really cut it off?" Jasper asked with disbelief.

I shrugged my shoulders, "If needed."

I could see him wince at the thought.

Caspian grabbed glasses and a bottle of scotch off the side table and sat on the couch, "So what are we going to do? We can't leave in the morning as planned. They will spot us before we can get there."

I ran my hand down my face and leaned back against the leather sofa.

"We could go west?" Leo suggested.

"It's too close to the humans," Caspian replied.

"I wouldn't be surprised if he left out a few scout locations. No, we need to be more cunning. We must find a way to sneak off of pack lands without alerting them," I said, taking a glass of scotch from Caspian.

"Can we leave a few at a time?" Jasper asked.

"They would take notice," I countered. "What about a truck?" You have cattle; do you have a rig we can haul men out with?"

"Not a bad idea. But it wouldn't fit enough of them," Caspian added.

He sat back and took a sip of the amber liquid as he thought.

"Groceries," he sat back up. "We get our groceries delivered. I can send June into town tomorrow and see if she can rent the truck. It's only a box truck, but we should be able to get quite a few more warriors in it."

"Do you think they would rent it to you?" I asked, hopeful.

Caspian chuckled, "If the price is right, I don't know how they could refuse."

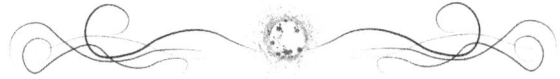

18

Juniper

"Make sure to stick together," Forest said as he helped pull on my jacket.

"I know, Forest. Do you really think they would try something in town?" I said, trying to ease his worries.

He looked at me seriously, "At this point, I wouldn't put anything past them."

"Time to go," June called out from her Suburban's driver's side door.

We were in the garage where they stored all of the cars. Four warriors were hiding themselves in the back. I looked back at Forest with a reassuring smile before I stood on my toes, pressing my lips against his. With our unspoken farewell, I walked around the car and climbed into the front passenger seat. The floor had a backpack with $50,000 in cash in it. I had no idea a pack would keep this amount around, but the more I thought about it, the more it made sense. If there were ever a time that the pack was discovered or needed to flee, they may not have time to stop at a bank. We took off down the gravel drive, turned onto the paved main road, and left the pack lands behind us.

"What reason are you giving the manager for needing to rent out the truck?" I asked June as we traveled down the road.

"I've thought of a few reasons, but I settled on the story that we lost power to our freezers due to the fires, and we want to rent it for the day to keep our food fresh."

"Is it a refrigerator truck?"

"It is," she smiled at me.

"Why didn't we just rent a truck? Wouldn't that have been easier?"

"They would notice a truck coming onto our property. The grocery truck already comes every week. Having it come and go wouldn't be odd, just a normal event in our routine."

"Makes sense," I said as I leaned against the window, watching the towering mountains pass us.

"How are you boys doing back there?" June asked as we pulled into town.

"A little cramped, but we'll live," Silas, one of the West Moon warriors, replied.

June laughed, "Only a few more minutes and you can slip out."

We pulled into the parking lot of the local grocers and June parked in between two cars. I climbed out of the car and looked around to be sure no one was watching. We had to be certain that the rogues weren't keeping tabs on us. Without finding any suspicious eyes, I opened the back door, and two of the four warriors slipped out, staying hidden between the cars. The other two climbed out on June's side.

"You guys know the plan. Juniper will return to the car when we need Jared to come in," she reminded them.

"Yes, Luna June," they acknowledge.

I pulled the backpack on, and June and I entered the store. For being bright and early, I was surprised by how many people were already doing their weekly shopping. A handful of checkout stands had people manning the registers with a small line at each one. Several other people pushed their squeaky carts up and down the aisles. I looked around, taking in each passerby. Knowing that the rogues had been watching us made me skeptical of even the most normal-looking people here.

I continued to follow June. She obviously knew where she was going as she walked down the front past the registers to a worn-looking door. A window was next to it with binds opened, viewing a slightly chaotic office. An elderly balding man with wide-rimmed glasses sat at the desk, busy with some paperwork. June knocked a few times, and the man looked up. June smiled, and he waved us in. We stepped into the cramped office and closed the door behind us. There was one spare chair across the desk from him. It was a brown course material with once-padded arms.

"Good morning, June. What can I help you with?" he asked hoarsely.

"Hi, Bill. I have a huge favor to ask," June said with her straight-to-the-point attitude.

"Go ahead," he said as he sat back and placed the pencil he had been using down.

June sat in the worn chair and leaned toward him, "Have you heard of the fires at the ranch?"

He frowned, "I did. I'm sorry to hear of your loss. Do they know what happened?"

"Arson," she said in a mournful tone.

His eyes widened, "Wow! Who would have done something like that?"

June shook her head and gave her best, disappointing look, "We have no idea. They're investigating, but we can only pray that it never happens again or to someone else."

Bill shook his head with distaste at the action.

"Anyway," June added, "the reason I'm here is to see if there is any way we could rent the delivery truck for the day?"

Bill cleared his throat and leaned forward, holding his hands on the desk, "I'm sorry, June, but we are not allowed to rent it out."

June held her hands against her chest and nodded solemnly, "I understand. I had just figured I'd ask. The fires caused the power to go out at our main house. The freezers were cold enough to keep the food cool yesterday, but the power company will not make it out until tomorrow morning. I had just thought that if we could use your refrigerator truck, we wouldn't have to throw all our food away."

Bill rubbed his chin, "I really wish I could help you. That's terrible."

"I understand. I even brought cash to pay you upfront on the off chance that you would be willing. Thank you anyway," she said as she stood back up.

She began to turn towards the door. My feet stood still at how easily she was willing to let our plan slip away, but just as she reached for the door handle, Bill stopped her, "Well... Maybe we could work something out."

June turned back and smiled, "That would be great. How much are you thinking?"

He ran his hand down his chin again as he thought it through.

"Perhaps, $5,000?" He offered a little too eagerly.

Her face beamed, "Of course. I know it's an inconvenience for the store."

He smirked, "Oh, you know. These things happen sometimes."

June turned towards me, "Juniper, why don't you get the cash for me."

I grinned at her as I headed back out to the car. I pulled out $5,000 from the backpack and slipped it back on, sliding the cash into my pocket. When I walked back in, I heard Bill and June laughing.

"There you are, Juniper. Did you have any problems?" June asked me.

"No," I smiled back, handing her the money.

Bill's greedy stare eyed the stack of cash as she slid it onto his desk. He picked it up and ran his finger through it, counting it as he went.

June picked up the keys from his desk, "We should have it back tomorrow morning."

"No problem," Bill replied, his eyes still on the stack of cash.

There was a knock at his office door and he shoved the cash into one of his drawers as he looked suspiciously out the window at the man.

"No need to worry about him," June reassured him. "That's my ranch hand, Jared. He's here to drive the truck for me."

His suspicion waned, "Oh...okay. You already have the keys. We may need to unload any groceries they've already loaded on it."

"He will wait. I need to get back. There's a lot going on trying to get us back up and running after the fires," June told him.

"I understand," he smiled. "You have a good day, and you know our number here if you need anything else."

"I do. Thanks again, Bill," she said, smiling before turning toward the door.

We returned to the car, climbed in, and left the parking lot. The other three warriors would head out to scout ahead for us while Jared would bring the truck back. Once it was there, we would quickly load everyone in and send out the first crew. June pulled out her phone and called Caspian.

"We're good to go. See you soon," she told him.

She hung up and placed her phone in a cup holder in the center console.

"I thought you were going to walk away when he said no," I laughed at her.

"You have to hint at what they can get but not be scared to walk away. That's what gives you the power in negotiations," she smirked at me.

"You're a smart cookie," I teased her.

"And a sweet one at that," she laughed in return.

We drove down the twisting mountain road, heading back towards the pack lands. We were close to halfway when I caught the hint of a shadow in the trees nearby. I watched out my window, trying to make out what it was. With the continuous attacks on the pack, we were all on edge. It was a good mindset to be in as I realized it was a dirtied sandy brown wolf racing to keep up with us.

"June, we have rogues," I warned her hastily.

She peeked out my window, but the road's curvature meant she could only pay attention briefly. She pressed on the gas, the engine roaring as we hurtled faster down the road.

"We should be close enough to the pack. Let them know," she said as she watched the road.

"I don't think we should."

"Why not?" she glanced at me surprised.

"Forest said that they were trying to lure the warriors off the pack lands so they could attack. This could be what they are trying to do," I explained.

"Talk about a smart cookie," she smiled. "This car should be able to outrun them. We just need to make it back."

As we charged down the road, I spotted three more wolves joining the first.

"There's more of them," I informed her.

"They won't be able to keep up for long. The road straightens ahead, and we can get away from them," she said, her voice calm.

As we turned a sharp corner to the right, one of the wolves dashed in front of the car, but June never let off the gas. We felt a hard thud, and the vehicle swerved as she righted herself, slowing down to regain control.

"Why would they do that?" I screamed.

"They probably assumed that we would have hesitated. They don't know who they're messing with," she said with determination.

The road straightened out as she had said, and she floored it. The remaining rogues trailed behind and finally disappeared amongst the trees. We slowed down just before the turn-off onto pack lands. Several warriors were busying themselves near the entrance, waving us on as we passed. As we navigated the interior roads, we passed the housing where a fire department pickup truck and a police car were parked. She slowed down and rolled down her window.

"Any news?" She shouted at them.

The two men were standing near one of the burned buildings. At her shouting, they walked up to our car.

'Mornin'," the police officer said as he tipped his hat. "What happened to the front of your car?"

He walked to the front of the suburban and looked it over. June hopped out and joined him, "I hit a deer on my way home. I figured I'd send some of the boys back to clean it up."

"That can make for some good meat if it's salvageable, not that you're lacking in that department, though," he told her.

"Never hurts to add to it," her welcoming smile returned.

"No, it does not," the officer said, patting his belly.

They walked back to the side of the truck, and June hopped back in.

The police officer leaned on her open window, "Anyway, to answer your question, it looks like whoever started this threw some liquor bottles lit aflame through the windows."

June played it up as she gasped and held her hand to her mouth, "Who would do such a thing to us?"

"We're still looking into it. It's a good thing you had your gathering last night," he said thoughtfully.

"I am so grateful. These houses are full of families. I couldn't even imagine what would have happened if the children were home. Do you think whoever did this knew they would be empty?"

"Perhaps," he said as he ran his tongue across his teeth. "We will let you know as soon as something comes of it."

"I appreciate that. Thank you, boys," she smiled as she rolled up her window and started back down the drive.

As we pulled back into the garage and parked, I asked her, "Do you think we should let Jared know about the rogues on the road?"

"I already did," she said, tapping the side of her head. "I don't think they will give him any problems. They won't know he's part of the pack. Nonetheless, I told him to keep an eye out just in case."

19

Forest

I was angered that Juniper neglected to inform us that the rogues chased them from the town until they were back to pack lands, but I understood her reasoning. It concerned me that she would hold back from telling me if she were in a dangerous situation to keep me from coming to her. No matter how often I explained it, she never entirely accepted that she was my priority. There would be other opportunities for us to take down the rogues or whatever adversaries we would end up facing, but I would break without her. I knew without a doubt in my mind that without her, my heart and body would die. How can one still walk the earth with half of your heart ripped from your body? I needed her. She was the drive behind everything that I did. The swiftness of my feet... the skill that I use to fight... the voice in which I led with... No matter the consequences, I could not risk losing her.

I took a long, frustrated breath as I pushed through the

garage door. I would be riding in the back of the box truck while Caspian would be in the cattle trailer. They would follow us out in an hour so as not to raise suspicion. We would converge south of the lake where the rogues were camped. From there, we would sneak up and circle their camp, finally wiping them and their unhinged minds from the earth.

Juniper walked up to me with a concerned look. It was the same one she gave me each time I left to deal with some form of danger. My heart ached, and I felt her worry, but it was necessary to protect her and her family.

"Fight sure and brave," she said to me.

And be careful. I love you, she linked after, keeping her worry between just the two of us.

I love you too, Juniper. Promise me you will contact me if there is a problem.

Her vibrant green eyes looked up through her thick lashes as me, *I will, I promise.*

We loaded tightly into the back of the box truck, shoulder to shoulder. We wanted to fit as many warriors as possible without revealing our movements. We had to ensure the group was not alerted to our plan. The engine spurred to life, and we rolled out. Our tightly packed bodies helped support us against the bumps and curves of the rough roadway. When we finally reached the smoothed pavement, we serpentined down the mountain road for nearly an hour. The plan was to cross through the town before heading to our destination. This ensured that anyone watching assumed the truck was returning to the grocers as usual. The second truck would head north and loop around, heading to our rendezvous point.

With a hard turn, we ended up on another unpaved road.

This was our cue that we were nearing our destination. With a sharp squeal of the brakes and a jostle forward, we came to a stop. The driver, one of the Silver Ridge warriors, walked around the vehicle, scoping out the area before knocking twice on the metal siding. He unlatched the lock, and the doors pulled open. The bright, blinding light made my eyes squint as they adjusted. We all piled out. I shouted directions to set up a perimeter, and the men quickly carried them out. I called over a small group of warriors, a mix between the two packs.

"You six run up ahead, find our scouts, and keep an eye on their camp. Report any movement and look for their trails," I directed a group.

"Yes, Alpha," they returned before turning to prepare.

The other truck should be arriving within the next hour. It was a waiting game until we could join the two groups and push forward. We busied ourselves to set up a rudimentary base camp, using the truck as a command center. A folding table with a map of the area was set up in the center. Caspian and I had already drawn out our planned movements for our warriors to study beforehand. A small generator had been packed on the passenger floor of the cab. With it, we could run spotlights into the back of the truck to illuminate the darkened space. There was not much need to have the plan all laid out beforehand as we had gone over it in detail before we left, but we were taking no chances.

The roar of a semi's engine pulling itself down the uneven dirt road pulled all of our attention. A cloud of dust rose above the treetops as it navigated the path. We were fortunate that the road did not have tight turns leading to us. Otherwise, they would have needed to abandon the rig and run in on the main road. If one of the rogues spotted it, our position and element of surprise could have been given away. Our knowledge of their camp's location would be rendered irrelevant.

The truck parked parallel to ours, hissing as the brakes engaged. One of the warriors ran towards the back, opening the door. The sides of the truck, which was made from perforated slats of metal, had tarps covering the inside to conceal the men. One after the other, they piled out, stretching their limbs before joining the rest of us. Caspian was one of the first out.

"Any tails?" he asked me.

"No, not that we noticed," I replied.

He gave a curt nod, "Good. Same for us."

We stepped into the box truck and stood on opposite sides of the small table.

Do you have eyes on the camp? I linked Parker, one of the scouts.

Yes, Alpha. We have a count of thirty-three so far, but we could have missed a few sleeping in their tents. Their camp is one hundred yards south of the lake, hidden amongst the trees. They have makeshift tents scattered throughout a fifty-yard area.

There were fewer than the captive rogue had told us. I could attribute that to their own scouts and patrols being out. We already knew where they watched the pack from. Jasper was leading a group to eliminate them as we spoke. I could sense his eagerness to prove himself to his father. Any other unaccounted-for enemies could have been killed during yesterday's attack or asleep in their tents, as Parker suggested.

Let us know if there are any changes, I told him.

Yes, Alpha

"They're here," I informed Caspian, pointing to the map.

I went over the details Parker had passed to me.

"I'll come in from the east. You take the west," he said.

With the plan in place, we reiterated it to the awaiting warriors. Four groups were already assembled. Caspian, Oakley, Beta Leo, and I would each lead one. I stood on the edge of the truck so everyone could see me.

"This is it," I started speaking to the warriors. "We all know the plan. We close in on them. Keep the perimeter tight. We don't want any slipping past us. We have been through one hell of a week with each other. It's time to bring peace back to both of our packs."

They all nodded and grumbled in agreement.

"Let's go get them," Caspian called as he shifted, tearing away his clothes.

I held back my smirk at his showmanship and slid my clothes off, unwilling to destroy my last pair of pants. I felt the electric charge in the air as I shifted into my black wolf. I was the largest wolf there, even bigger than Caspian's chocolate-brown wolf. Without waiting another moment, I darted off into the surrounding trees, my group of warriors hot on my tail. We moved swiftly but silently as we made our way across the two-and-a-half miles of rugged terrain that separated us from the enemy.

I could smell the foul scent of rogues before we even sighted their camp. It lingered in the air, marking their established grounds. We slowed our steps, taking every precaution not to alert them prematurely. Parker's light-colored wolf came up on our side. He shifted into his human form before going down on one knee by my side.

"They have three guards patrolling the perimeter," he shared.

I nodded at one of the Silver Ridge wolves, telling him to

pass the information to Caspian and the others. We had a series of wolves assigned to relay information between the groups to keep the line of communication open.

I want four on me; the rest of you hang back until you see the signal, I linked to my warriors.

Parker relayed the information to the Silver Ridge wolves, as our contacts in the other groups did the same. Confirmation came through that the others would follow suit to take out the patrols. I stayed low as Parker led me to the right. I caught sight of the first patrol walking the edge of a ridge. They had the uphill advantage, making it difficult for us to approach undetected. Due to the need for communication, I only had my own warriors with me.

Heath, create a minor distraction behind those boulders, I pointed my snout to the left of us.

Yes, Alpha, he said before sneaking off to the side.

We need to be quick and silent. We can't let him call out a warning.

The others nodded their heads.

We moved as close as we could without giving ourselves away and waited. There was a sound of a rock tumbling behind the boulder to our side. The rogue's head perked up, watching in the direction it had come. Hidden by a few nearby rocks and trees, we watched as it slowly approached the boulder. Once it was past us, we silently moved in behind. Its wolf sensed us and whipped around. Without hesitation, I leaped forward, clutching his throat on my jaws and clamping down as the first howl of warning had attempted to escape. I tore my teeth through its flesh, ensuring my kill. I dropped the limp body, and it landed with a thud at my feet.

I called the all-clear, and the rest of my group joined

back up with us. We stalked to the top of the ridge, giving us a clear view of their camp. There was no sense of order to it. Tents made from sheets and tarps were slung up to trees with fraying rope. A few campfires were lit while most were left waiting for use. A small group was sitting on a felled tree, and another was facing them. They were lost in conversation about non-important matters. Most of the rogues sat silently on their own. It was obvious that being in a group was foreign to them. Most would have likely been rogues for many years. Being thrust into any form of social setting again would leave them unsettled.

When we received word that everyone was in place, we waited for Caspian's signal. The call came through the link, and we began the charge. The once nearly silent area, void of the typical serene music of nature, erupted in chaos as the sound of sixty sets of thundering paws made their way down the ridge, directly at the rogue camp from all directions.

The ragged-looking men I had been watching quickly jumped to their feet and shifted. A howl echoed through the air as they tried to warn everyone, but it was too late. It was only a matter of seconds before we reached them, claws and teeth slicing through flesh and fur like butter. A mangy-looking black and brown wolf with a light-colored face advanced toward me. It reared back, slicing its claws at my face. I dodged its attack, swerving to the side. I pushed off my rear feet, lunging at its flank. The coppery taste of blood oozed through my mouth as I ripped off a chunk of his shoulder, spitting it to the ground before taking another pass at it.

Without the ability to put weight down on his front leg, he slowed in his maneuverability, making it an easy task to finish him off. I latched onto the back of his neck, crunching down until I heard the distinctive sound of bone breaking. His body went limp within my jaws, signifying his death.

We swept our way through their camp like a wildfire amongst a field of dry brush. With the sounds of battle waning, I stepped back and took in the scene. Bodies were littered amongst the trees, blood soaking the earth. As far as I could tell, we had not lost a single warrior. Our precise planning and tactics led us to victory. I shifted back so everyone could hear me.

"Keep one or two alive for interrogation," I instructed.

Caspian's wolf trotted up to me, shifting in step. He stood at my side, observing our warriors. Creature turned into man as they each shifted back. A few stayed in their wolf forms and trotted off to begin patrolling the area. An order given by one of the Beta's, I was sure. Two injured rogues were hauled to a nearby tree, where they were bound with some cordage scavenged from one of their makeshift tents.

"Check the bodies," Caspian called. "I want Callan found."

I agreed with his order. If we failed to capture Callan, there would be no stopping him from forming another rogue army. He had been driven mad from his banishment and the loss of his mate. The Silver Ridge Pack would be at risk until he was dead, his body buried deep in the earth.

"Successful attack," I said to Caspian as I watched the warriors begin to collect the dead.

They would be hauled back to the pack to be burned. Usually, an honor that is only given to our own, but with so many bodies, it would be too great of a risk to bury them throughout the forest. We did not need someone stumbling upon their remains. It has happened in the past from time to time and usually results in an investigation by humans. They could pass it off as an animal attack since that is what the wounds would show, but the act of burying the body showed human involvement, or so they said. If we left them out in the open, wolves would be hunted down to take out the risk of a repeated attack. Humans were so clueless, yet we had to live by the restrictions their societies placed on us. They outnumbered us millions to one.

Beta Leo jogged up to us and lowered his head to Caspian, "I'm sorry, Alpha, but there is no sign of Callan."

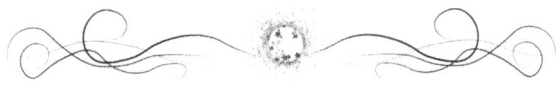

Juniper

"**C**ome help me with this roast, dear," June said, busy at work at the kitchen counter.

I walked over and stood beside her, "I'm sorry I'm so useless right now. I always worry when Forest is off fighting."

"We all do, honey," she smiled compassionately at me.

"I don't mean to be so selfish when I say that. Of course, we are all worried."

She stopped what she was doing and turned to look at me, putting her fists on her hips, "There is nothing selfish about it. I don't want to hear you talk like that again. Do you understand?"

I nodded as my eyes widened at her response. Her face softened, and she turned back to the slab of meat in front of her.

"I'm just saying that we all feel that ache deep inside our souls when our mate is in danger. You are still young, and your bond is new. It will affect you more. As time passes, you will find what helps you calm those nerves of yours."

"I hope so..."

"I like to keep my hands busy, hence the roast. Why don't you start cutting up the carrots and potatoes."

I walked to the other counter and grabbed the large bowl of washed carrots before returning to her side. I pulled over a cutting board and peeled the carrots, letting their trimmings fall into a second bowl. The kitchen was fairly empty at the moment. It was only June, myself, and two other women at work. She was right. My mind eased as we busied ourselves preparing dinner, and I fell into a steady rhythm. Once the roasts had been assembled and tucked into the hot ovens, we began whipping up some custard for dessert.

"Ladle it into each cup and set it on the tray," she instructed as she continued prepping the berries that would go on top of it.

I had only lifted the ladle to the first cup when I heard Bryony gasp behind me. I quickly turned around and spotted a man who had just entered through the back door. He was covered in filth and reeked like a rotten rabbit that had sat in the sun for a few days. He had a hold of Bryony by the throat as he stared us down.

"Callan, you let her go right now!" June shouted at him.

She clutched the small paring knife in her hand. A look of readiness was in her eyes as she waited for an opportunity to attack him. I took in the appearance of the man again. This was Callan...the man who had organized the group of rogues and had attacked my family's pack again and again. His face was familiar as I recognized him from his visit to our pack. A fire began to form in my gut as anger swelled within me. He was the reason my mate and my family had to continually fight for their lives.

"I will not," he smirked at her, drawing my attention back to him. "You see, your mate has attacked my group. Luckily for me, I have been keeping to your borders, just waiting for an opportunity like this. He killed Abigale. I planned on avenging her death with your own, but I heard that the West Moon Luna is also his daughter. Is that why we were called to your pack?"

A pregnant moment of trepidation filled the room.

"Anyway, it doesn't matter," he scoffed at us. "I figure, what better way to make everyone pay? Kill the Alpha's daughter and the Luna of the other pack. The one that had me banished."

He leaned down and ran his nose up the side of Bryony's neck, never taking his eyes off me. When he reached the top of her head, he squeezed Bryony's throat even tighter. She gasped in the tiny air she could as her face flushed a deep red.

"Now, here's the situation. You can come with me will-ingly, and I will spare June and his little peach right here. Or you can fight, and I will crush her windpipe right now before killing both of you."

Bryony's feet lifted into the air as he suspended her. Her face began to turn blue from the lack of oxygen.

June put a restraining hand on my own, urging me to stay quiet, but I could not let someone else be hurt protecting me.

"The warriors are already on their way," June smiled at him. "You won't have a chance to escape."

"I don't need to escape. I will kill her before they get here," he smiled wickedly at her.

I saw the pressure increase on Bryony's throat, and I could take it no longer. I stepped forward, "I will go with you. Let her go."

"Juniper, no!" June protested.

He released Bryony, who fell onto the floor unconscious. I could hear the labored breaths from her telling me she was still alive.

"We leave now," he demanded.

He took two steps forward, grabbing my arm roughly and pulling me towards the door. I considered fighting against him now that Bryony was free, but the twenty remaining guards had been posted at our borders to ensure the rogues would not get onto the territory. I had no clue how Callan had slipped past them, but he would be familiar with the ins and outs of the pack's workings. June would have linked them when he entered, alerting them, but it would still take them another five to ten minutes to get here. In that time, there is no saying what a vengeful, crazed former warrior would do. I was sure that June was a tough fighter, but men led for a reason. They had superior strength. It was the natural order with us. A battle with Callan would most likely result in injury or even death of at least one of us. If I could get him to leave, I could use my fire against him. I could not risk burning down their pack house by fighting back now.

"I would kill you here, but I want to take pleasure in the torture I will bestow upon you."

His foul, hot breath made my skin crawl.

June stepped forward, preparing to rush at him, but I nodded and mouthed "*Trust me*" at her. She hesitantly stood back, but I could see the fight within her. He dragged me quickly out the back door and shoved me in front of him.

"Run," he demanded.

I started to sprint away from the house. I did not intend to stray too far, but I would need to face him in order to cast the spell. With me being in front, he could take me down before I could properly invoke the incantation. I allowed us to travel a ways into the forest, but not wanting to go any further, I dug my feet in and turned to face him. He never faltered at my sudden stop, and instead, my eyes landed on his fist, slamming straight into my face. I fell backward, stars lining my vision. My head was in a fog of disorientation.

When the fog began to lift, I realized I was tossed over Callan's shoulder, bouncing against his back. I could hear my warriors calling out to me through the link.

We're coming, Luna, they said.

I tried to bring clarity to my thoughts, but I was tossed to the ground roughly. My shoulder slammed against a tree, sending a sharp pain shooting through the limb.

"I had hoped to enjoy this a little more, but it looks like this is as far as you go," Callan looked at me with disgust.

He walked up behind me and grabbed hold of my head with one hand on my chin and the other around the back of my skull. I immediately knew he intended to break my neck. I had no time to call out a spell. This was it.

Feel it, Selene's voice shot through my thoughts in a split second.

As if it made perfect sense, though I did not understand why, I felt my power surge and a force blasted out from me. Callan hurtled backward, slamming into the ground fifteen feet away. He jumped up, startled, and looked around.

"What the hell was that?" he grunted as he stormed back at me.

I clenched my fist, feeling what I could only describe as

his spirit within it. His feet halted, and his arms held tightly to his sides.

"What are you?" He spoke with disdain.

I watched as he fought, feeling only a slight push of pressure against my grasp.

"You have caused enough strife for one lifetime. Your journey ends here."

I sent a wave of my power at him, feeling it flow out of me like water gushing down a waterfall. I could see the sparkling blue light traveling the distance between us. It entered his body, his face contorting in pain and agony. Only a moment later, he exploded from within. Chunks of Callan flew through the air, landing in every direction. As I saw a piece coming my way, I raised my hand to block it, but a shield of icy blue air formed before me, stopping it in its path.

What had just happened? I looked around at the carnage. The largest piece that remained of him was no more than the size of my hand. I had no clue I could wield such power. I didn't even know something like that was possible. There was always an incantation when magic was cast. Words were to be spoken. A request, a wish for Selene to grant. When I heard her words, I immediately knew that I had to feel the power within me. With my desperate need for Callan to release my head, it pushed him away as if answering my plea for help. I was at a total loss at what I had just done.

Before I could spend more time trying to solve the puzzle in my mind, I heard the approaching storm of paws. They slid to a stop as they found me, looking around at what remained of Callan. They looked at me with shocked stares. Their reaction was not a surprise. No witch that I had ever heard of before wielded this much power. Not even the dark witches who offered blood sacrifices to grow their abilities.

Colt, one of the West Moon warriors, shifted, "Are you alright, Luna?"

"I-I am..." I stuttered.

"I didn't figure you needed much help, but this," he looked around. "This is something else."

I looked up at him with the same look of surprise, "I guess so."

"We should get you back to the pack house."

"Yes... we should go."

I could feel the slight unease in the air. I was unsure if they were taken aback by what was left of Callan or if they were uneasy with me. I know I would be cautious if I saw someone who could do such a thing as I just had.

Not wanting to strip down to shift, I walked back. Colt shifted back into his wolf and circled me along with the other nine warriors. I needed time to piece together what had transpired to understand what all of this meant. I was utterly lost in my thoughts as we trailed back the way we had come. I felt my power within me. It felt more potent, more alive. I could feel it coursing through my veins like a current. Even with such a heavy use, I hadn't been weakened. I fiddled with my fingers as my mind raced. I could feel a charge build in my fingertips from the action and quickly stopped. I couldn't risk sending it out. I felt both entirely in control and without any control of my power simultaneously. The back of the pack house came into view as we descended from the trees. June raced towards us.

"Juniper! I am so happy you are alright," she called as she widened her arms to pull me into a hug.

I stepped back, worried that my power would zap her. She looked surprised but lowered her arms.

"What happened? Did he hurt you?" she asked concerned.

I couldn't even begin explaining the events I had just partook in.

"No, I...I just need some time."

She looked at the warriors, who were shifting back into their human forms. Other women had come out with clothes for them to change into. They avoided her glare, not wanting to speak of what they had seen.

"Someone better tell me something," she demanded, her hands back on her hips.

"I took care of him. It was just more than I have done before."

Her frustrated look transformed into that of confusion.

"Please," I looked at her with pleading eyes, "just give me some time."

She pursed her lips but stepped aside. Cain and Oliver stood at the door, watching with curious expressions. I made my way to an unoccupied door and whisked inside to the safety of my room.

21

Forest

Caspian and I returned to our base site and waited for the warriors to finish cleaning up. They were hauling the bodies to the semi, where they would be transported back to the pack. A team would be staying behind to sanitize the area. The two captives were to be brought back in the box truck for further questioning. We had sent out scouts to look for Callan. He had somehow evaded us, but we would not rest until he was found.

"Alpha's," one of the Silver Ridge warriors called as he jogged over to us from the box truck. "There's news from the pack. Callan attacked the Lunas!"

"What?" We both growled in unison.

"He has taken Luna Juniper."

My wolf surged forward, shredding my clothes as I took off towards the pack lands. While it was a reasonable distance away, it would take longer to get there with the truck, and I risked being pulled over by a human police officer if I sped. In addition to the speed restraints, the rogues were tied up in the box. That would land me in their justice system, something I couldn't risk. I could hear Caspian trailing behind me. We wove through the small valley that led back to Silver Ridge land. When we had closed the distance enough to link with the pack, I reached out to my warriors, who had remained there.

Where is your Luna?

We're trailing them now, Alpha. They can't be more than a mile from us, Colt responded.

Get to her now!

Yes, Alpha.

Anger, frustration, and worry filled me. Callan should never have been able to get to her. The patrols were supposed to have stopped anyone from getting into the territory. My legs burned as I pushed them, but there would be no letting up.

I felt a sharp pain radiating from my face, and I immediately knew that it was Juniper. Fire swelled inside of me, and I imagined every last thing I would do to Callan to make him suffer. No one hurt my mate. Once and for all, he would pay with his life—a renewed energy burst within me. I was unsure if it was my desperate need to reach Juniper or something else. It felt like nothing I had experienced before. I pushed myself harder, faster. I had to get to her now!

We have her Alpha. She's safe.

Thank the goddess! Colt's voice seemed to lack confidence in the statement, but I would figure that out when I arrived. Knowing she was safe, I felt a weight lift off my shoulders, but I did not let up. She needed me.

Get her back to the pack house. Does she have any injuries?

No, Alpha, he said, but again with hesitation.

What happened?

There was a slight pause before his response, *You are going to have to see it for yourself Alpha. I-I think she blew him up.*

I slowed for a split second as I took in what he said. How could she have blown him up? None of this made sense. We made our way through the southern border and bee-lined it to the pack house. June was pacing out front, a look of concern on her face. We shifted back as she handed us each a pair of sweats.

"What happened?" Caspian asked her.

"Callan came in through the back door in the kitchen. He nearly killed Bryony, but Juniper offered herself up," she answered, her voice filled with worry.

I growled in frustration.

June, understanding my aggravation, attempted to explain it to me. "She did it to save Bryony."

"Where is she now?"

"She's hidden herself away in her room. I don't know what happened out there, but something has unsettled her. She kept her distance when she returned, and the warriors refused to tell me what happened," she said.

"You didn't force them to?" Caspian asked, surprised.

She gave him a hard stare, "I figured that if they felt the need to hold back from me, there was a reason."

With no sound answer to what had transpired, I moved around June and hurried inside and up to our room. The door was locked when I tried the handle.

"Juniper, let me in," I called through the door.

I could hear the light shuffling as Juniper climbed off the bed and walked to the door, unlocking it. Her face looked tired and dirtied. I scooped her into my arms and inhaled her scent deeply. She winced slightly, and I pulled back.

"You're hurt," I said, alarmed.

"It's fine. My shoulder got knocked into a tree, but it's already healing."

"What happened?"

She looked at the open door behind me. I stepped in and closed it. We walked to the bed and sat side by side. I held her hands tightly, showing her my support.

"Do you feel it?" She whispered.

"Feel what?"

"The power in my hands," she said with uncertainty.

"I don't feel anything abnormal."

A look of relief flooded her face.

"She spoke to me again. Selene. Callan realized he wouldn't be able to escape, so he tossed me to the ground. He wrapped his arm around my head intending to break my neck...and then she spoke to me," she sputtered with bewilderment in her voice.

A slew of emotions twisted inside of me like a hurricane. Relief that she was safe, anger that Callan had put his hands on her. She hesitated for a moment before continuing.

"For whatever reason, her words awoke something inside of me, Forest," she said, finally looking at me. "It was like an increase in my power, a new development. I didn't need to cast a spell, but simply think what I wanted."

She told me what had happened. I was taken aback when she explained what her power had done and the ease with which it had done it.

"Why are you hiding away now?" I asked her softly.

Her face contorted as a fear settled in her, "I don't know how to control this. What if I accidentally hurt someone?"

"You said that it does what you want, right? As long as you don't want to hurt someone, then I doubt you will," I tried to reassure her.

"I don't know, Forest," she replied, unconvinced. "I didn't want to blow up Callan, but I did. I just wanted to stop him, the same way as when I set fire within the wendigo."

"So you know that whatever this is, it works differently. You just need to train with it."

She bit her lip with nervousness. I spent the next hour soothing her concerns. She opted to stay in the room for the night. She was too wound up from the stress of the day. I needed to meet with Caspian and have a look at Callan's remains to get a better understanding of what she described. Though I knew she would have preferred me to stay with her, she understood my responsibility to attend to the Silver Ridge pack. I made sure she was settled before I left. I ran into Oakley on my way down.

"How's Juniper doing?"

"She's a bit unsettled. Bring her up some food. She's going to stay in for the night."

"Right-e-o captain."

Oakley was right back to his usual ways with the elimination of the rogue threat. I knocked on Caspian's office door and entered after he answered. June was seated on his sofa inside.

"How is Juniper doing?" June asked concerned.

"She will be fine. Something happened with her power, and it has made her a little uneasy."

"Is it what she did to Callan?" Caspian asked quietly.

I was sure his warriors who had helped retrieve her had filled him in.

"Yeah," I said, taking a seat. "It was a first for her."

"Caspian told me what she did. That poor girl," June said sympathetically.

I assured them, "It will take some time for her to accept it, but she will be fine. "

"Did she tell you what happened before she...dismantled *him*?" Caspian asked, searching for a word to describe it.

"She said he had his arm wrapped around her head, prepared to break her neck when she felt a surge of power."

I wasn't sure if they knew Selene had spoken to her before, so I omitted it from the conversation.

"Not surprising," Caspian sipped the amber liquid that swirled in his glass. "Her body defended itself. It's the fight or flight instinct but on another level."

"Yeah. Anyway, I'm going to head out to the site to see it for myself."

Caspian put his drink on the table, "I'll join you."

"I'm coming too. I need to know how to help her," June said as she sprung up.

Caspian put his hand on her knee and said, "No, dear. I think it would be best if just Forest and I went."

She huffed but sat back down, grabbing his glass off the table and downing it in one go. "Fine, but you better let me know what I can do."

"I will," he smiled at her as he leaned down and kissed her head.

I had Colt lead us to ensure we went to the correct location. He had already witnessed the scene, so I didn't need to worry about him. It was just over five miles north of the pack house. I could smell the early stages of rot as we approached. I saw bits and pieces of Callan flung throughout the space. Pieces were caught in the trees and scattered across the ground.

"Colt," I said as I shifted back into my human form, "you can head back."

He nodded his head and took off in the opposite direction.

"I guess we can be certain he will never bother us again."

I ran my hand down my chin, taking it all in. This was more than a small pop of the body. It looked like a bomb exploded from within him. The debris field was at least twenty feet wide and, by the look of the trees, equal in height as well.

"Has she ever done something like this before?" Caspian asked.

"She burned a wendigo from the inside last winter, but nothing like this," I explained.

He looked at me, "A wendigo? I didn't think those were real."

"Me either until one nearly killed me," I growled.

I could tell he was storing that in the back of his mind to ask about at another time.

"You said she felt a surge of power?" He asked.

I nodded, "That's what she said. She only needed to think of what she wanted rather than casting a spell like usual. Even with the fire, she had to chant to make it happen."

He scowled, "Power like this could be dangerous."

My hackles were raised at the insinuation that Juniper was dangerous.

He raised his hands defensively, "Not her. Well..." he lowered his hands back down. "Yes, she is dangerous, though I'm not worried about her hurting anyone. I'm saying that many in this world would do whatever they could to get a hold of a power like this. Try to control her for their own purposes."

I ran my hand back through my hair. This was something I had already thought about. She would be a prize to be captured.

"I don't know if anyone could control her with this new power," I said, looking around again.

"If there's a will, there's a way. Look how easily she gave herself up for Bryony. She is selfless. All someone has to do is find something to use against her, such as yourself."

Dammit. He was right.

"I would never let that happen," I said sternly.

"You just never know, Forest. What is certain is that we need to keep this under wraps. I have already commanded my pack not to speak of how Juniper healed the others, but I will put an Alpha command on them to forbid them from speaking of her powers at all," he tried to assure me.

I sighed, "Thank you, Caspian."

"She is my daughter," he said sincerely.

"She is."

"We will need to get a group together to clean this up. Though the scavengers should take care of it, it's outside our borders, and I don't want a human stumbling across it."

"I agree. I can have my men do it."

With our intentions clear, we turned back for the pack house.

22

Juniper

I awoke wrapped tightly in Forest's arms. His long, even breaths told me he was still deeply asleep. I inched my way out from under his arm that was draped across my body and headed for the bathroom; when I returned, he was sitting up in the bed.

"Should we grab a shower and then breakfast?" he asked groggily.

"I don't think I want to go down there."

"You can't hide away. You need to show everyone the confidence you have about your power. It will assure them."

"But I'm not confident," I argued back.

"Fake it until you make it," he smiled at me.

I shook my head and smiled back. It seemed like every other day when we descended the stairs and into the dining hall. There were a few more stares than usual, but they didn't linger. We joined my dad and June at their table. June jumped up at our approach and hugged me tightly.

"I'm so glad to see you, Juniper. You're one tough little lady."

Warmth spread throughout my chest. The insecurities of how everyone would see me after doing such a thing seemed unfounded. I had been deeply concerned that they would look at me like a monster. It was, after all, something I was battling within myself. It wasn't so much that I had killed Callan but rather the method with which I had done it. My newest surge of power scared me. I still didn't know if I might accidentally hurt someone.

With spells, one had control of their magic. I had to focus and channel the spell through concentration and words to enact it. With Callan, I simply thought it. What if I was mad at someone and wished that they would trip? What if I wished for something worse... Would it happen? Would my will push my magic to ensure my wishes were granted, even if said through the heat of emotion?

I forced a smile at June now that my mind had gotten away from me once more.

"It's good to see you too."

With the tension lifted from my shoulders a bit, we enjoyed our meal. Many of the Silver Ridge pack members came to thank us for our help in protecting their pack. The gratitude and appreciation they showed us filled my heart with warm happiness. Forest looked at me with admiration as I talked with each person.

The overwhelming sense of rejection I had feared I would receive that morning, to my current state of complete acceptance helped to create a new sense of determination. I knew that my newfound skill set would need to be honed and mastered, but I had come to realize all of the good that I could do with this. I would no longer worry about how I could help contribute to protecting my pack. If a band of rogues invaded our pack house as had happened to the Silver Ridge pack, I had the capability to stop them and hopefully prevent loss within our own pack.

"I would like to go back to the coven to talk to the elders about the evolution of my power and see if they can help me train," I told Forest when we returned to our room after breakfast.

"Then we will make it happen," he said with assurance.

His eyes softened as he looked at me. He stepped forward, his arms wrapping around me like a comforting blanket.

"Is this something that we can wait a few months on? I hate to ask this of you, but we have been away from the pack for a while, and I need to be there for them. For at least a month or two."

The familiar anxiety of accidentally injuring someone reignited deep in my stomach as I thought about his request.

"Can we stop there on the way? I want to ask them about it first and see if they can offer me some guidance before we head back."

He exhaled, accepting, "I think we can manage that."

"Thank you," I whispered, resting my head against his firm chest.

WE SAT in my father's office along with the high ranks from both packs. June sat upright next to my dad. She was sipping on a cup of hot tea I had made her. She had come to love my combination of herbs, and I had promised to prepare a batch for her before I left. Jasper, Oakley, and Beta Leo leaned against the walls in one place or another. Forest and I sat on the perpendicular leather sofa as we reviewed the events involving Callan's rogues. I had come to learn the standard practice of debriefing after situations. It was a time to come together, reflect, review, and find ways to improve from events and situations.

"We obviously have some flaws in our perimeters. Twice, the rogues were able to sneak past our patrols. Not counting the times that they outright killed our warriors," Caspian commented, the hint of anger and frustration heavy in his voice.

"I could put up a ward? It's what we did at my coven," I offered.

"What would that entail?" June asked.

"I would need to walk the perimeter while reciting an incantation. I think I can specify that it only affects those who intend to harm you. It would steer them away from here, but they wouldn't realize it was happening. More of an instinctual deterrent for them," I explained.

"They wouldn't know what was happening?" June asked further.

"No, they would feel uneasy or confused if they tried to pass through it. Eventually, it would feel like there was a wall there if they pushed hard enough, but they wouldn't be able to understand what the barrier was. At least not, unless they were familiar with spells. If it were another witch, she would be able to sense it."

"Walking the full perimeter would take you at least a day or two. Can you do it as your wolf? If so, that could cut the time down significantly," Caspian asked.

"I think walking in my human form would be best. I would want to be sure that it is done properly."

"Do you have a day or two to spare?" Caspian directed at Forest.

"I will send the majority of my warriors and Beta Oakley back today. Juniper and I can stay to be sure that the ward is in place if you would like her to do that for you," he said.

"It will not affect our people, correct?" Beta Leo added.

"As long as they don't intend harm on the pack or its members, no," I confirmed.

"Then I would be thankful for your help with it. We have lost too many already, and we will need time to recover and rebuild," Caspian looked at me with solemn appreciation.

The strain on the pack had become more evident as the dust had begun to settle from the whole predicament. Families remained close to the pack house, fearful of wandering too far away from its unspoken security. Warriors were often on alert, snapping their hard, suspecting gazes to the slightest movement. Even my father had evidence of the impact it had on him. His forehead bore a few more wrinkles from countless hours of frustration and worry. My heart felt for him. For the whole pack.

"I understand," I said softly, followed by a pause. "It would be best if I return once a year to restrengthen it. It loses its vitality over time."

I would do anything to protect them from this ever happening again. To have them witness such hardship.

"Another reason for you to visit us," June smiled at me.

AFTER LUNCH, Oakley and all of the other warriors, minus five who would be staying with us, left for the airport. We all said our goodbyes. The entire Silver Ridge Pack that had been available showed up to wish them farewell and express their gratitude for all of their help. My heart swelled with both pride and happiness that we were able to help them. To make a difference.

After the large black SUVs disappeared in the distance, only a cloud of dust lingered in the air. My dad and I walked down to the entrance of the ranch. My father would join me as I set the barrier to be sure I stayed on their boundary. Though, as a wolf, I could sense the edge, it was still helpful to have someone familiar to keep me on track as I focused on the spell.

We spoke of small things, the weather, June's cooking, and the plans for the community building back at our pack. Things that held no weight as both of us still felt the heaviness of the last week on our shoulders. As we approached the tall wooden posts that jutted out from the ground, marking the entrance, we stopped.

"If you lead, I will follow after. I won't be able to talk while I'm casting, but we can stop for breaks," I told him.

With a confirming nod, I began the incantation low on my breath. I could feel the electrical charge swell within me and push out as I started. The cool early summer breeze nipped at my cheeks and blew my rich, currant red curls into my face. I felt the slow trickle of magic flow out from within me as I stepped one foot in front of the other. We moved slowly but intentionally as we traveled the unseen line that separated the Silver Ridge pack from the surrounding forest. We stopped after the first three miles. My dad handed me a bottle of water he had carried.

"It's remarkable what you are able to do with your powers," he said casually.

I looked up at him and wiped the water off my lips, "I'm just happy I can help you."

Half his mouth curved up in a cocked smile, "I know we have only just found each other, but I want you to know that I am proud of the woman you are."

His words struck me with surprise. Compared to June, I felt like I had a lot to learn. I was still figuring out how to bring my pack together. To create that inner security that she brought effortlessly to Silver Ridge. As I focused more internally, I realized that my father saying those words swelled my pride. I knew my Gran had always been proud of me, but having the approval of a parent was foreign to me and something that seemed to hit a little deeper than even when Gran said it.

"Thank you," I said sincerely.

He grinned at me before taking a swig of water. We returned to our task. I followed his lead as we made our way through the thickening trees, finding a trail as we went. Besides the few breaks we took, we never faltered and were able to complete our tasks by dusk. When I pulled the two seams of the ward together, sealing them, I could feel it arch upwards and curl inwards as if an invisible dome had been placed over their land.

"Anyone within the ward will feel a pressure if someone tries to pass it."

"The whole pack?" he asked.

"Yes, as long as they are on pack lands."

"That's amazing," he said with aww.

He turned back to me and half-smiled again. When it was just the two of us, he seemed to grow at ease. I could tell

he had let his hard shell as Alpha drop, and it warmed my
heart that he was comfortable with me enough to do so.

With the ward in place, we returned to the pack house in
search of dinner.

23

Juniper

Same as the day prior, when we said our farewells to Oakley and the other visitors, the majority of the Silver Ridge pack had shown up to see us off. I was overwhelmed with their kind words of gratitude. I had expected a small crowd since they already shared their heartfelt thanks the day before, but as we walked out the front of the pack house, we were confronted with a wall of people all there to say goodbye to us. I shook hands and hugged each one as I passed. I felt a connection to the Silver Ridge Pack. Whether by blood or from enduring hardship together, the bond had been formed, and I would forever feel it with them.

When I came up on Fleur and Daisy, a tall man stood behind them, holding onto her shoulders. Fleur's eyes were glassed over from unshed tears as we approached.

"Luna Juniper, we are forever indebted to you for coming to Fleur and Daisy's aide," the man spoke sincerely.

"There is no need to be indebted. I'm just glad I was able to get there in time."

"You are wrong. Luna June told us how you had no hesitation when you heard that they were out there. Without you, we all would have died."

I knew that he was referring to succumbing to the loss of his mate. He, too, would have perished from their loss. A heartfelt smile came to me as I hugged each one of them. I saw June and my dad standing at the end of the line of people and approached them.

"Goodbye, Juniper," June said, pulling me into her tight embrace. "You have been a light brought to us. We love you, sweetheart."

"I love you too."

As I watched the swirling cloud of dust fly into the rich robin egg blue sky behind us as we drove off, I was filled with mixed emotions. Their sincerity and praise touched me. Confidence in myself grew, pushing the doubt I had embedded within what I had done to Callan out. While it would still take time to digest the fact that I had detonated a man with my powers, I realized that I was capable of not only defending myself but of protecting those who were weaker. I abolished a man who wished harm to others in this world. Because of my actions and the actions of the warriors who fought so gallantly against the rogues, the world had become a little brighter and safer for everyone.

I watched the towering mountains cascade past us as we followed the serpentining black river of asphalt back to the airport. The few stray clouds in the sky looked like water churning in a river—the rapids of the sky. My thoughts reminisced on our time at the Silver Ridge Pack. There were many highs and lows on which to reflect. My life had changed drastically since I found Forest. If you had described to me what it would have been like, I would have been scared to face such challenges. Now that I had walked these steps and experienced it all, I was grateful. While I lived in peace at the coven, my life had been bland. The same tasks and chores day after day, month after month. I could have told you what each of my coven sisters was doing at that moment. Life was predictable and something I was happy to move on from.

I wished there was a way for them to spread their wings and find paths to tread outside of our hidden sanctuary. A way for them to grow into something greater. Perhaps this was something I could bring up with my Gran during our visit. Maybe we could welcome coven members up to the West Moon pack. We could teach them the ways of our world, and they could help around the pack, creating a relationship between the two.

The brakes gave a light squeal of protest as we pulled into our parking space.

"You have been quiet on this drive. Are you doing alright?" Forest asked me as he lifted my hand to his lips, lightly brushing them against my pale skin.

"Yeah," I said, looking over at him, "I just have a lot on my mind."

"Are you still worried about your power?"

"Yes and no... I need to learn how to control it. I need to learn more about it, but I have realized it's not something to fear. It's something to embrace."

I could feel his lips curve up into a smile against my skin.

"I'm glad to hear it. I agree with you. You are a force to behold, Juniper. There should be nothing about you that you feel apprehensive about. You are nothing but perfection."

"So much flattery," I joked with him.

"Just speaking the truth, my wildflower."

WE PULLED into the parking area of the coven in our rented car. Forest had sent the warriors back home to reunite with their families and take a well-deserved rest while he escorted me to the coven. I had called Gran from the Durango airport to let her know that we would be coming for a visit. The call had been short, and I could not fill her in on what had happened, so it was no surprise when I saw her standing at the top of the hill waiting for us, a look of concern in her eyes.

"Gran," I said as I approached and wrapped my arms tightly around her.

While I felt a new bond and connection with my father and his family, I could never forget the arms of the woman who had raised me. She had comforted me after each fall and scrape, soothing me back to sleep after a nightmare. Her embrace was more of a homecoming than the coven itself. She held me tightly—longer than our usual greeting—and could sense my need for her.

"Come on, dear. Let's get you two settled," she said as she took my arm in hers and led us through the settlement.

Looks of surprise and welcoming glances came from each face we passed. Gran had obviously not informed the others of our arrival yet. We passed over the small wooden bridge that connected the two sides of the creek, which ran through the middle of the homes, and followed the trail past the Nary home to my mother's house. An aromatic soup was cooking on the stovetop, filling the space with the scent of herbs and rabbit- my favorite dish and comfort food. This was precisely what I needed after the last week.

"Come have a seat," Gran said, gesturing to the table.

Forest took our bag to the bedroom as Gran, and I sat across from each other.

"Tell me what's going on. I can see it in your eyes. Something's happened."

I took a ragged breath in. While I felt accepted at the Silver Ridge pack, the life of a shifter was drastically different from the coven. The women here were a peaceful community. They would have to understand that it was a matter of life or death and a choice I had not even realized I was making.

"Gran," I looked up at her, knowing she would accept me no matter my actions. "Something happened with my power."

EPILOGUE

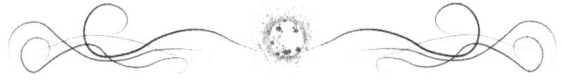

Juniper

I pulled the stubborn carrot from the earth's hold and added it to the wicker basket next to me. I stood up and brushed the dirt from my flowing green cotton skirt before lifting the basket and walking down the row of vegetables.

"Luna," Holly, one of the other garden workers, lowered her head as I passed her.

"Hi, Holly. How is the cabbage looking?"

"Good, besides all of these pesky caterpillars," she said as she picked one off and added it to a glass mason jar to her side.

"They're just looking for food. Make sure to get them to Oliver before you leave so he can release them up in the valley."

"Yes, Luna."

I smiled at her, knowing her annoyance was kept at bay. Holly despised bugs, yet Oliver liked to allocate her to collect them off the vegetables. She must have done something to insult him at some point, as he was one of the most passive men I knew. I pushed open the garden gate and loaded the basket filled to the brim with realgar orange carrots, their green stalks flowing over the edge, into Oliver's old truck bed.

"Are you done for the day, Luna?" Oliver's deep, shaky voice said from behind me.

I turned to face him, "I am. Do you need anything else done?"

"We're just about finished here. The girls will take care of the rest."

I looked back at the bountiful gardens that sprawled across the land. The gardens were always among my favorite places to help at the pack. I loved to sink my fingers into the rich, moist soil, helping to sprout new life. Over my time there, I cast spells upon the land to ensure the best crops. The plants that had already been fruitful were now bursting with abundance. Oliver had hired five new pack members to help keep up with it all.

"Let Oakley know if you need anything while I'm gone," I told him.

"Of course, Luna. Thank you for all of your help, as usual," he smiled at me.

"It's you who we should thank. You do an amazing job keeping up with all of this."

We parted ways, and I strolled back to town, picking a few wildflowers from the roadside on my way. As I neared the first few buildings, Forest's chiseled face came into view.

"What are you doing out this way? I thought you were meeting with the warriors?"

"Already done. I thought I would walk with you."

"That's a welcomed surprise."

He joined me and laid his heavy arm over my shoulders as we continued. We waved hello and greeted each person we passed as we made our way to the cafe. I ordered my usual tea, which was now a top seller with my concoction of herbs that I supplied them. Tea was always better when made from scratch rather than the prepackaged stuff they used to buy in bulk.

The steam tickled my lips as they hovered over the cup. I took a slow sip of the fragrant liquid, its warmth tracing down my insides until settling in my stomach.

"Are you ready for the trip?" Forest asked me.

"I think the bigger question is if you are? Are you sure you will be able to handle two weeks away?" I teased him.

"Oakley has it covered. If anything happens, I can return in a few hours," he answered casually as if the idea of being gone for a few weeks wasn't bothering him.

We had been gone a lot over the last year. I knew he had responsibilities at the pack and had sacrificed so much for me already.

"And the plan if it takes more than two weeks?" I asked, looking up at him.

"Then August will join you until I can return," he assured me.

I took his hand and said, "Thank you for making sacrifices to come with me."

He squeezed my hand back, "I would do anything for you. I'm just appreciative that you waited these last few months so we could get the pack in order."

"Gran gave me the tools I needed to control my power until we could return."

"Yes, yes, your daily meditation," he cocked an eyebrow at me.

I lightly smacked his arm, "You could do it too. At least it seems to have calmed the power inside of me."

"I think it has helped with your worry. I don't think you can calm the power. It's always inside of you."

"Yes, but the meditation helps me control it."

"Whatever it takes to help you, I'm on board with."

"Thank you," I said stubbornly to him.

Forest tightened his hold on my arms, reassuring me.

"How do you think the coven will react when they learn of my new power?"

"I think you're the better one to answer that question."

"When Pearl learned that I could perform beatha gealaich she started to call me the chosen one. I don't think this will help with that."

"What if you are the chosen one?"

I stopped cold and looked at him with surprise.

"Do you think I am...a *chosen* one?" I asked nervously.

"I don't know, Juniper, but you have done things I didn't even know were possible. You're powerful. You need to learn more of your powers and what you are capable of," he answered honestly.

I chewed on my lip, "I can agree that I'm powerful, but I wouldn't go as far as calling me chosen."

"All I'm saying is that you need to keep an open mind. There has to be a reason why the moon goddess has given you so much power. You told me that she came to you when Sienna stabbed you. Have you ever been able to hold another conversation with her?"

I shook my head, "No. Not a conversation. I believe she talks to me, but it's just words on the wind," I explained.

"Perhaps that is where you need to start. Find a way to talk to her and let her tell you what she has in store for you."

"I don't have any idea how to do that."

"Hence the trip to your coven. For how much I want to be the one to help you answer all of your questions; this is in the realm of the Wiccans. Only they can help you learn how to harness your power and perhaps even speak to the moon goddess."

I rubbed the side of my face as a new uncertainty settled within me.

"You're right. I will speak with the elders first thing tomorrow. I guess that's the best place to start."

Forest leaned down and kissed my forehead.

"Just remember that I am right here with you, and I always will be."

FOREST WAITED outside the large wooden double doors as I entered the hall. We had driven down to the coven yesterday afternoon and enjoyed our evening dining with my family. Today, I confessed my power to the elders, hoping they could guide me on how to control them better.

The six elderly women were along one side of an old long table. They quieted with my approach. I stopped before them, standing as tall and confident as I could portray.

"Thank you for seeing me," I told them.

Pearl, who had become the head elder after my great aunt Violet's banishment, welcomed me.

"Tell us why you requested this meeting, Juniper Nary," she said easily.

"Something has happened with my powers."

"Have they waned?" Autumn Martin asked.

"We have wondered how they would be affected by you pairing with a shifter," Hazel Murphy added.

"Let her finish," Gran scolded them.

"No," I said quickly. I cleared my throat as I continued, "They have grown."

Their curious eyes studied me as I stood vulnerable before them.

"Tell us more," Pearl instructed.

"As many of you witnessed when the wendigo came here, I have been able to summon stronger power within me. A few months ago, something happened, and now I can call upon my powers at will."

"As can we all dear, what makes you think they are growing?"

I bit my lip. This was the moment that I would confess that my power now surpassed their own. Would they see me as a chosen one like Forest predicted? Or would they look down with judgment as if something was wrong with me? Would they question whether I had ventured into the dark arts? At least my Gran stood amongst them. I was not alone.

"I no longer require incantations to summon it. I can merely think of what I wish to happen."

Silence filled the room for a moment as they took in my words.

"Can you show us?" Pearl asked. "Light a fire in the fireplaces."

Behind them, on the towering wooden planked wall, sat two fireplaces on either side. There were stacks of wood held in black metal holders to the side of each of them. We usually only used the fireplaces in the cold winter months when the added heaters would not suffice to warm the ancient dwelling.

I looked back at Gran, who gave me a reassuring nod. I focused on the wood, willing it to lift from its holders and move into the fireplaces. I could see the shimmering edges as my power floated away from my body and drifted across the room, wrapping itself around the logs. They lifted into the air before landing in the metal cradles inside each of the fireplaces. My power tightened its hold before a burst of magic ignited the logs into a roaring fire.

I looked back to the elders, all of whom were twisted in their seats, watching the flickering flames dance. They slowly turned back to me one by one, each with a look of disbelief. Gran unsuccessfully hid her grin of approval.

"You really are the chosen one, Juniper," Pearl whispered.

AFTERWORD

Thank you for investing your time in reading The Wiccan's Circle. Your support, whether through sharing with friends and family or leaving a review on Amazon, is greatly appreciated. Authors like me rely on readers like you, and your actions can make a significant impact.

Thank you again. To read more of Ayla's books or learn more about her current projects, visit her website at www.aylavolk.com.

Until we meet again...

ABOUT THE AUTHOR

Ayla, a passionate reader and author of shifter and fantasy romance novels, is known for creating strong female leads. Her novels are not just stories but empowering journeys that delve into the strength women possess. Her character development is her strength, and readers will love getting to know them better and being able to invest their time into their tales.

ALSO BY AYLA VOLK

The Stolen Heart

Warriors of the Eclipse

The Warrior's Calling (Book 1)

The Warrior's Bond (Book 2)

The Warrior's Proving (Book 3)

The Hunted (A Side Story)

The Wiccan Saga

The Wiccan's Alpha (Book 1)

The Wiccan's Hunt (Book 2)

The Wiccan's Circle (Book 3)